MARRANGA LIMGA

FAYE ROOTS

Published in the United States of America

ISBN 978-1-970703-24-5 (Paperback)

ISBN 978-1-970703-25-2 (Hardback)

ISBN 978-1-970703-26-9 (eBook)

For Book Rights Adaption and other Rights Permission.

Call us at toll-free **601-914-6178**.

# Contents

The past is the doorway to future hope.

CHAPTER ONE

ARRIVAL

THE HORSE SNICKERED. Its tail constantly swished at the cloud of flies swirling around its rump. It was very hot and the wheels of the dray jarred dustily over the pitted, uneven surface of the dirt road. Cicadas screeched in ear-splitting discord while overhead a flock of galahs complained bitterly at all the interruptions.

Robert Barritt fanned his face with his hat. 'Whoa!' He directed the horse to the sheltered shade of nearby trees. He dropped the reins and wiped the perspiration from his face, trailing fingers through his tangled black beard.

'Almost there,' he said to the woman in the seat beside him. 'Don't know how the little fella can sleep when it's this hot so early in the day.'

He smiled across at her and gazed fondly at the curled-up form of his two-year-old son on the woman's lap.

Eliza tried to engender some enthusiasm in the smile she reciprocated. She still felt homesick and longed for the security they had left behind in Brisbane.

'Almost there,' Robert announced again proudly.

Her heart dropped and she actually felt quite sick. *This gift, this legacy his uncle has bequeathed – eighty acres of cultivated farmland and a house on the banks of a river – it sounds exciting. But here ... why here? A mining settlement. A gold rush town. What future is there for us here?*

Twenty-one-year-old Eliza Barritt, three years younger than her husband, was a tall slender woman, with a head of heavy dark brown hair. It fell to her shoulders, struggling to escape from the straw hat anchored not too securely by a long hatpin. Even while seated in the dray, she held herself erect with dignity. Her appearance, frail beside her husband's bulk, disguised a strong will and determination. She was dressed in a high-necked, long-sleeved blouse and ankle-length skirt. On her feet were the handmade tan leather boots her father had given as a parting gift. She was hot and very tired. She unbuttoned the first four buttons of her blouse and fanned her hot, perspiring neck. 'No sign of any houses yet,' she said, surprised. 'I thought we would have reached the borough centre by now.'

'Over the next rise, love.' He couldn't keep the excitement out of his voice. 'Only another half a mile and we'll be there.' He wondered how she was really feeling. He knew the separation from her parents was hard. She had cried, but in that stoic way of hers, she had said defiantly, 'If it's what you want, then I'm beside you. You're my husband and where you go I will follow. I'll help you in every way I can.' He was pleased but at the same time hoped she would be happy. Just being with him was not enough. He wanted her to be happy and feel like she was 'coming home' as well.

Once long ago – or so it seemed now – he had stayed at the cabin. He remembered fondly the river, the swimming, the laughter, and the games with his cousins. The sense of accomplishment was great when they had planted the first vegetable garden. He remembered when James Nash discovered gold and the thousands of people who came looking for instant wealth. But that was all in the past now.

On this steamy January day in 1880, he wondered again, as uncertainty filled his mind, if this was the right decision for his family. The death of his uncle and two cousins, followed by the news of the unexpected inheritance, had all happened very quickly. Now here they were. The future was both exciting and frightening.

'Enough rest,' he called out to the horse 'Gee up! It's time to be going.'

The wheels of the dray renewed their desultory cycle and the swirling dust once more coiled behind them.

Suddenly, they were there.

Mary Street, a straight yellow–brown dirt road, brooded over by huddled buildings on both sides, looked alive in the early morning sunlight. People scurried everywhere. Smoke billowed from a campfire somewhere in the distance, and there were breakfast smells coming even from what looked like shopfronts.

Shops, houses, temporary wooden shelters, and even a tent or two were clustered together, as if for security and warmth. There was a sense of permanence now. It seemed the flood of 1870 had fired an enthusiasm to be more established for the future.

Robert found a holding yard. It took some time.

There was a constant milling of people and horses, and he simply continued driving until he found a cleared area. He released the horse into an adjoining enclosed paddock and pushed the dray against the back paling fence.

'Come on,' he said excitedly to Eliza. He helped her down. 'Let's go for a walk.' The child woke with a petulant cry. Unhappy about the disturbance, he began to yell, thrashing his arms and legs wildly.

'Shush. It's OK. Everything's OK. Mummy and Daddy are here.' Robert took the little boy's hand. 'Come on, Son,' he said, laughing. 'You can walk with me. This is Gympie. This is where we're going to put down our roots. We'll take a look, then go on to our new home.'

They walked on together. Curious eyes followed them everywhere they went. A few people waved and smiled, but most were occupied with their own daily activities. Some gave penetrating stares before quickly returning to their duties.

Shops were opening and displays of fruit and vegetables in wooden crates spilled out on to the narrow footpath. It was easier to walk on the road, and Robert directed his family carefully, avoiding horses and carts and milling people.

'Ah, the top of the mornin' to yuh,' a voice suddenly called from the small alley beside a solid square timber building. A bank sign gently swayed in the breeze. 'New around here, aren't yuh?'

Robert nodded. 'I'm Robert Barritt and this is my wife, Eliza, and son, Joel. We're going to be living a few miles down the road on this side of the river.'

The man moved out of the shadows. He was a large, stocky man but gave the impression of being much taller than he actually was. His face was large, sun-burnt chestnut. His powerful jawline projected proudly its display of bristling inky black, red speckled beard. His dark eyes flashed with intensity. Hatless, his thick head of fiery red hair caught the sunlight and dervish-danced with life and vigour.

'Michael O'Reilly,' he shouted into the atmosphere. 'It's pleased I am to meet yuh.' He extended his large hand and squeezed Robert's with enthusiasm. Robert secretly wondered if his fingers would ever return to normal. 'And this, this is my wife Mara or Marrangaroo – it means little blue flowers.' Arm outstretched, he gently drew a woman and child from out of the shadows to his side. 'And … and before you think or say anything, she really *is* my wife. Father McMurtrie can confirm it.'

Eliza and Robert smiled at the Aboriginal woman. She was tall, almost as tall as her husband, dusky black with a coal sheen polish to her skin and hair. Her tightly curled hair was very short and her eyes shone like black agates. She smiled shyly at them and glanced affectionately up at her husband.

It was the child who clung shyly to Michael's hand that completely took Eliza's breath away. Young, probably ten or eleven years old, the girl was extraordinary. She was beautiful. Thick golden yellow hair – the colour of ripened corn – spilled on to her shoulders. Copper skin and tawny eyes shone with health and intelligent vitality.

Robert tried to keep his astonished eyes from looking at her too intently.

'This …,' said Michael, proudly tugging at her hand and drawing the girl closer, 'this is our daughter, Nika.' He smiled down at her.

For a moment, he stood there holding her hand defiantly, feet firmly set slightly apart, daring them to show by expression or action any disapproval. His free hand clenched threateningly at his side.

'What lovely dresses,' Eliza's voice broke through the tension. Mother and child were dressed simply in loose-fitting, straight from the shoulders dresses that fell without waistline to their ankles. They were both barefoot. The fabric, a very soft cotton–linen weave in a rich orange–brown colour, was unusual.

'My mother sent them from Ireland,' Michael said briskly. 'Now, would you like us to show you a little of the town?' He moved slightly ahead, his arms enveloping his wife and daughter in a light protective embrace. 'There's not a lot to see, but we're becoming quite established now and you'll find everything you need. Three pubs and two brothels for a start.' He laughed. 'A bank's on the corner next to the hardware store, and practically everything else is scattered along the road's edge. What's not available can be ordered from Brisbane or someone could try to get it from Maryborough. You can catch a steamer from Noosa to Brisbane twice a week if you don't want to travel overland. (Good stables are right beside the wharf to leave your horse.) There're Chinese market gardens springing up all over the place too. If you're heading to the south side, you'll see 'em everywhere.' Michael grinned again. ''Tis better not to get on to the Chinese argument. There's some sayin' already we've got too many and they should go home. But what they say about me and my wife and family doesn't bear repeatin', so I say just let everyone be about their own business.'

He carefully edged around a dray parked on the street's edge. A man unloaded heavy sacks on to a pile near an open shopfront door. 'Good morning, Michael, not used to seeing you in town so early.'

'Yes, it surely is a good mornin'. The birds are singin' and folks like you is already workin.' Michael laughed up at the young man, who with sleeves rolled up was heaving at the heavy sacks. 'This here's Frank Turner. He owns the produce store.'

Robert extended his hand. 'Robert Barritt, my wife Eliza, and son Joel. We're taking a quick look round before heading out to our new home, my late uncle's place, a few miles down the riv …'

'Are you Jake Carswell's nephew?' Frank interrupted, surprised. He kicked the last bag down the back gate of the open dray and gave Robert his full attention. Robert nodded. 'Well, now I am pleased to meet you. It's saddened me to see the property unattended for so long. Not much land but a pretty place, "Jakdawn".'

'I didn't know the place had a name,' Eliza remarked, interested. 'Perhaps even your husband didn't know.' Frank jumped down and stood beside them in the street. 'A few weeks before he died, Jake made the sign. Guess it was his tribute to the past.'

'My aunt's name was Dawn,' Robert interjected gently. 'She died in 1869. No, I didn't know the place had a name. It still seems impossible that they've all gone now.'

'Yeah, we were all pretty upset about it when we heard. Half the mining team died. Some sort of fever. Jake and the boys had only joined them for a few days.'

Joel's restlessness became obvious. 'Come on. Come on,' he chanted. He tugged at Robert's hand and managed to slip out of his grasp. Eliza grabbed for his shirt, but he escaped and ran excitedly towards a brightly coloured display stand on the footpath.

The horse attached to the stationary dray turned his head as the child ran by and began pacing restlessly, snickering at a passing horse and rider.

Joel, unheeding and focused only on the bright objects of his attention, ran forward between the two horses. His small legs pumped with enthusiasm but were still slightly unsteady. He slipped, then tumbled right into the path of the large brown stallion's restless hooves. The dray horse quietened, but the stallion, alarmed, reared up, flashing hooves pawing at the open air.

Michael moved quickly. He lunged for the child and rolled. Locked in a tight embrace, man and boy somersaulted through the dust and slid into a grain sack with a loud crunch. They sat up white-faced and shaken.

The horse and rider moved on. The street returned to normal.

'You must watch the horses. Always keep your eyes on the horses,' Michael soothed the boy in his arms. His heart raced. He offered up a silent prayer, ''Tis grateful I am the child's not hurt.' Eliza, Robert, Mara, and Nika looked down, shock real in their eyes and etched on their faces.

'Oh, Michael, thank you. Sometimes he moves very fast.' Eliza picked the boy up and hugged him to her breast 'You must never run away like that from Mummy again.' She was sobbing and her shoulders shook violently with shock and relief.

Robert wrapped his arms around them both. He steadied her and spoke quietly and soothingly to Joel. One hand gently caressed Eliza's hair.

His eyes for a moment connected with Michael's. 'Thank you.' His voice was unsteady and slow tears slid down his cheeks. 'I owe you one, mate.'

'Ah, 'tis all part of the service.' Michael dusted himself down. He smiled, turned, and with Mara and Nika at his side walked back down the street.

'You must ride out and visit us in a couple of weeks,' Eliza called out after their retreating figures. 'We should be settled in by then. We'd love to see you.'

'If you're looking for me, you'll find me in the Royal most nights,' Michael shouted. 'That's the pub there behind you next to the grocer's store.' They kept walking and disappeared, presumably turning off and walking down the same alley from which they had first appeared.

Robert, Eliza, and Joel stood once more alone, feeling lost and shaken. 'What an amazing man! He seems to have disappeared as quickly as he appeared. Oh, Robert, Joel could have been killed. He could have been seriously injured.'

The three stood, quietly locked together for some minutes.

'All right if I give the boy a lolly?' a bright, cheerful voice called from a doorway further up the street. A well-dressed middle-aged woman walked towards them. She wore a high-necked white blouse. It was tightly belted at the waistline over a long dark skirt. The hemline swirled across the dusty walkway and only the tips of small booted feet could be seen.

'He hasn't had his breakfast yet, but thank you, I'm sure he'll enjoy it. He's had a fright.'

'Yes, I know,' the woman said. 'I saw it all from the window of my bedroom.' She waved her hand towards the house behind her and smiled cheerfully at them. 'I'm Kat by the way.' She shook their hands with a polite little bow. 'Once long, long ago in another lifetime I was Katherine, but everyone calls me Kat these days.'

'Good to meet you, Kat. I'm Eliza. This is Robert and our son, Joel.'

Joel turned and waved to the woman as they made their slow way back down Mary Street. They collected the horse and reattached the dray. 'Let's stop along the road and have our breakfast,' Eliza said, her voice still unsteady. 'I ... I ... I just want to get there now.'

A gentle breeze teased at the light wooden gate. It swung desolately back and forth. Unhinged at the top, it drooped tiredly. The sign '*Jakdawn*' was still readable, but the paint had already weathered and was peeling.

'One of my first jobs must be to fix that gate and restore the sign,' Robert remarked cheerfully. He gentled the horse as they drove carefully down the overgrown but still distinguishable dirt track to the hut. It sat only a few yards from the river. The river looked beautiful, a snaking ribbon of blue water. In the far distance, a line of green hills were touched with gold as the sun rose higher in the sky.

'This is certainly a beautiful place.' Eliza climbed down from the dray unaided and helped the boy to stand beside her. Robert laughed as the horse he had now freed galloped away. Age momentarily forgotten, it pranced and danced in the exultation of a new freedom.

The timber hut was sturdy and well constructed from logs. The timber roof struts were sealed with grey slate tiles. It had a compact kitchen area with a large black cooking pot hanging from a hook in the ceiling. The cooking facilities were primitive but adequate. A large metal disc, probably from a wagon wheel or plough, was anchored in a boxed stone recess. There was a pile of firewood stacked in the corner.

Two bedrooms and a small room with a table, two chairs, and two heavy lounge chairs completed the hut. Along the wall facing the river, a narrow wooden veranda extended.

Sturdy wooden shelves stacked with plates, cups, and cutlery lined one wall. A small rough-hewn table, piled with frayed and dusty cobwebbed books and papers, struggled to remain upright in one corner.

Both bedrooms had sturdy beds. In the larger room, a double bed that was made up and covered with a large handmade quilt had cobwebs extending to all four bedposts. Clothes still hung on a railing nailed to the back wall.

The small room had two single beds obviously handmade but supported by strong wooden cross-bar legs. These beds were covered with moth-eaten blankets. The rest of the room was bare.

Homesickness washed over Eliza. They moved inside, and Eliza swiped at cobwebs that clung to her face and clothes. 'Oh, Robert,' she sighed, 'there's so much dust and decay everywhere.'

Then she looked through the grimy window. 'There's a huge tank. We should have plenty of water. I won't have to wash and bathe in the river. I was a bit worried about that.'

Robert laughed. Joel skipped excitedly, his little legs dancing. The buckles on his blue trousers shone in the sunlight. He clapped his hands. 'Dis a nice 'ouse,' he said happily.

Eliza struggled to keep a pleasant expression on her strained face. 'There are better facilities here than I remembered,' Robert said. 'The shed out the back has a bath and you'll find stone tubs and a scrubbing board. There's a new shed now beside the stable. There might be some useful stuff in there as well.'

Noticing her unhappy expression, he went on, 'Tell you what, love, I'll set up the tent. It would probably be better if we lived there for a few days. I'll help you give the hut a good clean and we can move in when it's ready. We'll throw out anything that's not useful, and gradually we'll move our own things in. I think we can make it comfortable.'

He suddenly turned to Joel. 'Joel, you help Daddy put up the tent. I want you to stay near it. Don't touch anything but your own toys.'

'I'll clear around the hut, and I think it would be safer if I fenced it in,' he said to Eliza. 'Make it easier to watch for snakes and any dangerous spiders.'

She smiled hesitantly up at him. Once again her stomach heaved. A wave of heartsickness and doubt washed over her.

Am I really ready for this kind of life away from my family and friends?

CHAPTER TWO

MEETING PLACES

THE CROWDED, SMOKY room smelt of dust, sweat, and beer. Groups of laughing men crammed every space, their beers sloshing on to the dirt floor. Some were draped over the long timber bar while others jostled and talked in the overflow on to the street. The Royal Hotel was the watering hole and they gathered here en masse. They connected together – miners, railwaymen, farmers, local store owners, lease tenants from nearby holdings and property owners from further out in the hills.

'Has anyone seen Michael O'Reilly?' Robert yelled. He shouted louder, trying to make himself heard above the din. 'Michael, are you here?' Laughter, glasses clinking, and a few indistinct bawdy jokes were the only response.

Beth Masters, blonde hair tied back with a bright blue bandana, slammed a tankard of beer on the bar top. She hitched her dragging skirt to rest more comfortably on her ample hips and bellowed across the room, 'Michael O'Reilly, you son of a bitch, I know you're there. I saw you come in. It's no good hiding your red hair with that dirty hat of yours. I know you're there somewhere.'

'Oh! *That* Mike.' Suddenly, a voice spoke from the midst of a group of drinkers lounging against the back wall. It was Chas Ingott, the giant from the line gang. He was the brawn and muscles part of a newly recruited railways team.

He was very drunk and shouted again, his voice slurred and sarcastic, 'Oh, that Mike. He's the red-headed one with the Aboriginal whore wife, isn't he? The one with the black missus and the half-caste kid.'

'You got a death wish, mate?' Beth hissed across the bar. The warning came too late.

A body lurched through the door from the street and flung itself through the crowd. The swinging ceiling lamp directed a beam of clear light and the curly thatch of red hair stood out like a flaming beacon. A hat skittered across the floor and fell in the dust behind the bar. The bare head and a fist connected with Chas's chest and jaw. His body violently connected with the back wall. It vibrated. Tables overturned. Chairs upended. The smell of spilt beer mixed with general odours as men pushed, shoved, and fell over each other to get a closer look at what was now happening on the floor. 'Give 'em one, Mike,' someone called and several laughed drunkenly.

Michael had him by the throat and shook his head back and forth. The first fierce rush of anger passed. He swallowed, and then with a swift flinging movement, he dropped the heavy body with a snarl. Glasses and bottles shuddered on the bar.

'S'truth,' someone muttered.

'Yuh kin call me all the names yuh like and I probably deserve 'em all, but you'll show respect to my wife and child or so help me, as God's me witness, I'll thump the livin' daylights out of yuh.' Michael's fists were still tightly clenched. His eyes roamed the room and challenged anyone to disagree with him.

He saw Robert lounging against the bar and the faintest smile softened the brooding darkness of his expression. He tugged at his dark beard. 'Ah, 'tis yourself lookin' for Michael O'Reilly. Glad it is I am tuh see yuh again.'

Robert stepped forward, smiling. 'Look out, Mike!' he yelled. 'Look out!'

Chas's heavy-booted feet rose in an arc from the floor and connected with the back of Michael's knees. With a gasp, he toppled on to Robert and the two men smashed against the bar.

What happened next was total chaos. No one remembered later any clear sequence of events. Fists flew in all directions and connected with whatever or whoever was in the way.

Chairs, beer, glasses all became airborne.

Beth knew the safest place was on top of the bar. There she stood, skirt hitched, booted feet planted firmly, for the half hour of mayhem, until exhausted bodies finally fell in huddled mounds all over the floor.

In the morning, no one could believe the absolute carnage. Only the bar still stood, solid and ready for the night. The door was completely smashed and a couple of walls needed replacement.

Robert opened an eye, surprised to see filtering morning light shining through a chink between two buildings and on to the sprawled-out figure of Michael beside him. 'How on earth did we get here?'

'God's me witness, I haven't the faintest. All I know, lad, was when the bildin' looked like fallin' in on us, we ran like the dev'l hisself was chasin' us. Ah, 'tis not an altogether bad place to be at the start of a new day.' He laughed.

'I don't think Eliza's going to be very happy. She's probably been waiting for me all night. I expected to be home not much after midnight.' Robert heaved himself to his feet. He combed tired fingers through his hair and beard, yawned, jammed his hat back securely on his head, and walked with slow, uncertain steps to the stables. 'Wish I could remember exactly what happened last night. It must have been some party.'

Michael laughed again. He reclined back, his head resting on his clasped hands. He was comfortable and showed no sign of getting up. ''Tis probably better we don't remember. Somebody's got to pay for the damage.'

Robert turned back when he reached the building's corner. 'I looked for you last night to invite you to bring your family out sometime to see us. We're in the hut now, so you can come any day.'

'How's the missus?'

'Ah,' Robert hesitated, 'she seems happier now she's in the hut, but I know she misses her family very much. What about yours?'

'Oh, Mara's happy anywhere. A tent by a creek now that's home to us. The kid's even started school. I reckon we're all becomin' civilised.'

Robert laughed as he saddled up and began his ride home. 'Civilised, are we? After that riot last night, I'm none too sure about that.'

The argument continued through most of the day. 'You promised me you would never leave me alone at night except if it was urgent business,' she yelled. 'How was I to know you hadn't had an accident or something? Jake Barnes fell off his horse in the dark only last week and was dead when they found him in the morning. Surely, if you have to go into town you could try and get home before morning. Or better still don't go in at all. It's not as if you haven't enough to do.'

She slammed the door behind her and marched across the yard. Her anger clearly showed as booted feet pounded all the way to the lower vegetable garden. With her skirt pinned up somehow and defiant in the freer movement, she flung the rake to the ground and began digging with a spade. She was the picture of unapproachable fury.

Robert sighed. *What's the use trying to explain? I still can't for the life of me remember what happened after I punched some railway fellow who was clinging to Michael's back.* He shook his head and winced. *Perhaps I got hit on the head. I reckon we all had a bit too much to drink as well. How can I ever explain to Eliza when I don't even know myself?*

'You can come with me, Son,' he called across to Joel. The child watched sadly his mother's distant figure through the slats in the gate. The hut's surrounding fence certainly provided him with an adequate play area and a strong protective barrier against dangerous wandering near the river.

'Daddy's going to dig up some potatoes. You can put them in your blue bucket.'

Joel laughed. He ran to Robert, his tear-stained face now a beaming smile. 'My bucket's not blue – it's yellow. Silly, Daddy!' They cuddled, both smiling and happy.

The man and child spent a profitable afternoon collecting and storing potatoes. They laughed and sang and made a game of all their work. 'This is fun, Daddy.'

Eliza worked alone, until the late afternoon chill began to settle on the paddocks. Slowly and sadly, she returned to the hut. She prepared the evening meal and joked with Joel as she dressed him for bed.

'Good night, my little pumpkin.'

She was quiet and pleasant as she tidied up, but in the darkness, later that night, Robert heard her sobbing. He held her and spoke words of comfort and love. All she kept saying between tears was 'I hate it here. I want to go home.'

CHAPTER THREE

VISITORS

Eliza heard horses long before they reached the property entrance. She watched the riders negotiate the bush track from the hilltop gate and make their slow way down the incline to the riverbank hut.

Michael rode with straight-backed, almost arrogant dignity, with Nika in front in the protective circle of his arms. His black stallion dwarfed the brown mare ridden by his wife.

Marrangaroo also sat proudly with incredible dignity and grace. Eliza wondered if Michael had taught her to ride. If he had, he must be an excellent teacher. She rode with fluid grace. It is as if she and the horse were connected in spirit. She rode as if the two were one.

Eliza watched as Michael dismounted, helped Nika down, and then turned to assist Mara. She couldn't keep her eyes off the family. She had never seen an Aboriginal woman on a horse before. But then she had never known a family like this before. Mara was different from anyone in her previous sphere of relationships. Even Michael and Nika stirred her interest.

'I'm glad you've come,' she called from the veranda. 'You can tie the horses or simply let them run free. The outer paddocks are all fenced. Fyre will enjoy the company and the old mare won't even realise we've got visitors.' She smiled. 'Robert's with Joel in the bottom paddock. They shouldn't be long.'

Suddenly, she pointed behind them. 'There they are now. They must have seen you ride up.'

It was surprising how much they found to talk about. Michael was passionate about the future of the growing town and its surrounding farmlands.

'Ah, to be sure there's still plenty of gold out there too. It's in the creeks and waitin' for surface digging. I've got some claims staked all along the riverbank.' He grinned at Mara. 'If it's there, as God's me witness, I'm planning to find me some.

'There's a place in this community for us all. We need each other. We need the farmers for our food, the railway folk to complete that track from Maryborough. We need the mine development for future economy. We need the church folk for the nurture of our souls and folks like me that's keeps on lookin' for the golden dream.'

He took another sip from his mug of tea and grinned across the small wooden table. The dampened fire, inside the small recess, still smouldered.

'Yup, we're a growing community all right. We've cleared a plot for a proper cemetery now too. It's all about births, marriages, death, eternity, and the livin' of the life in between.'

He laughed loudly and exuberantly. Nika and Joel in the corner of the hut looked up. They laughed as well. Nika had been teaching Joel how to draw.

'There's going to be a wedding soon too,' Mara suddenly commented shyly.

'Yup! Our blonde barmaid is going to marry one of those railway blokes.' Michael winked. 'She's quite a woman, our Beth. She'll keep even one of those tough sods in line.'

'Who is she marrying?' Robert was interested although he had trouble even remembering her face.

'Ah, one of the linesmen, but his name escapes me. I think he's foreign.'

Eliza found herself gradually relaxing. The knot in her stomach dissolved. Companionship and the stories helped her feel part of the wider community.

'I would like to meet them all.'

'We will, love, we will.' Robert smiled at her. 'Now we're more settled we will spend time in town together.'

Afternoon shadows drifted their dappled tree shapes across distant hills, and the paddocks were softly shaded before the two families returned from a long afternoon walk. Nika and Joel flicked pebbles into the river. Their happy laughter was infectious and everyone smiled.

The horses obediently waited at the house fence. Michael's piercing whistle summoned them as the adults and children gathered to say goodbyes.

Marrangaroo suddenly stiffened. She stopped walking.

She turned and pointed back at the gently murmuring river, snaking in a gradual curve, a few yards below the hut. Her back was ramrod straight. She shuddered, her face a mixture of wide-eyed shock and fear. The fading sunlight shone on the ebony darkness of her skin and she looked timeless – frozen, eternal.

'What's wrong, Ma?' Nika moved to stand beside her mother. Gently, she placed a hand on her shoulder. Michael strode across and stood protectively behind them both.

Mara appeared unmindful of her family. Vehemently, she shook her head as if in anger at the river. Then she swung round in a full arc and pointed to the highest point in the far corner of the paddock. 'One day,' she said hesitantly. She struggled to find English words for her thoughts. 'Limga … will be limga.'

'What's limga?' Robert was interested. He moved closer. 'Mara, what's limga?'

'It means stone.' Nika who rarely spoke began now to interpret as her mother softly conversed.

'Mum says the river is very dangerous. One day it will destroy much. But she is sure that out of everything, even lots of sorrow, trouble, and strife, one day limga – solid, enduring – will stand up there on that high point. I'm not sure exactly what she thinks it will be, but she knows it will be beautiful and a blessing.'

'Sounds great to me,' Eliza laughed, a trifle nervously.

Michael moved closer to his wife's side. 'Careful, Mara. Careful, me luv.' He slid an arm across her shoulders. 'Don't say too much.'

Nika continued interpreting, 'I … I can't find all the exact words, but I think Mum strongly feels that out of a lot of unhappiness, not just here but in the whole community, there will also be a bright and enduring future.'

Mara looked down at her daughter and for a moment held both her hands.

'You!' Her voice now was very gentle. 'You will be the dream builder. You will build limga.'

Nika gasped. 'Mama, how will that be? How?'

Michael laughingly gathered his wife and daughter in his arms. ''Tis time we was goin'. Stories bin told. Time we was goin'. T'anks for your company and time.'

Robert stood at the house gate, one arm around Eliza and the other holding Joel's hand. They watched the O'Reillys ride up the hill. Michael waved enthusiastically as he refastened the top gate.

'I wonder what that limga business was all about.'

Eliza smiled. Robert realised she looked happier. 'I can't even imagine. But I do know this, unless I settle like a stone in this place and try my hardest to make it my home, I'll never be happy.'

'I promise I'll try harder too,' Robert replied. She hit him playfully on his backside and pulled his beard.

He chased her up the path to the hut and Joel followed laughingly behind.

The storm that night came with unexpected violence from the west, and although the rainfall was light, Eliza stood on the veranda and listened. The river murmured restlessly below. The jagged lightning flashes split the darkness and highlighted the highpoint, way up in the far corner of the land they had inherited.

Robert and Joel were fast asleep, but Eliza stood quiet and still.

She looked at the threatening sky.

'Limga,' she rolled the word on her tongue. 'Limga … a stone … stability.'

She pondered what the incident could really mean. 'Mara seemed so certain – afraid but certain. Marrangaroo and her vision of limga.' Eliza laughed up at the storming heavens. 'Marrangaroo and limga.'

'Marranga–Limga' – a new word came to her in a moment of inspiration. Overhead lightning slashed again and a crack of thunder reverberated along the timber veranda railing. She shook her head, puzzled. 'What an extraordinary name for something! Marranga–Limga. It has a prophetic sound. It's like a promise. Is it a goal for the future? Will it be the fulfilment of a dream?' She found herself suddenly praying. She remembered prayers from her childhood, and from somewhere there came this need to reestablish faith – to make contact with the God she had virtually forgotten in recent years.

'*O Lord*,' she cried into the crackling darkness. '*It's been so long. I need You. Please help me find my way back to faith. It's been so long. I need to know You're with me in this strange place. That You're with me in all the uncertainties the future holds.*

'Lord, please help me find again courage, faith, and strength only You can provide. If Marranga–Limga is something to come in the future, help me to live through the difficulties until the dream is fulfilled. In Jesus' Name. Amen.'

The next morning brought blazing sunshine and the paddock grasses glistened with the sheen of high moisture content. The sound of a galloping horse echoed clearly in the morning quiet. Eliza watched as the rider stopped in the top paddock and hitched his horse to a fence post.

He waved his large black hat in greeting and walked down the incline to the hut paddock. Wildly curling sandy blond hair blew in the light breeze and a cheerful voice called out, 'Hi! Hope you don't mind me dropping by. I'm Tom Daniels.'

Eliza remembered Michael had mentioned a young travelling evangelist was visiting in the borough. She wondered if this might be him.

'Hello,' Joel greeted Tom at the hut gate. 'I's Joel. Daddy's in the shed and Mummy's there.' He pointed.

From the veranda, Eliza called, 'Hello, come in. I'm Eliza. I'll put the kettle on.'

Robert found them seated at their small table, when he climbed the six steps to the veranda. He had washed some of the dirt off himself at the pump.

'Tea smells good, love,' he said, reaching for a mug.

'We've got bun,' Joel interjected.

'More like burnt damper,' Eliza shook her head. 'The fire was too hot.'

'Tastes great to me.' Tom's youthful face was tanned and cheerful.

Eliza was attracted to the mesmerising effect of his clear blue eyes. 'I'm simply riding around saying "hi" to folks.' Tom filled them in on his desire to help any families in the borough both practically and spiritually, if the need arose. 'I can't imagine life in this isolated community without God. We're a strange mix all right. We've got as many churches as we have brothels, and somehow we've all got to get along.'

'Eliza has always been the one with faith,' Robert commented as he slipped a gentle arm across her shoulder and moved closer. 'I've no problem if you encourage her and drop by some times, but I'll be more likely to be needing a hand in the shed.'

Tom didn't stay long on his first visit, but they found they really liked his company. He was an entertaining, energetic, enthusiastic young man. The Barritts, particularly Joel, warmed to him.

'My parents live in Sydney, but intend moving to Brisbane,' he told them. 'I have this strong feeling there is some sort of purpose to my life by coming here to this community. I'll be nineteen in two weeks,' he added shyly. 'I'm young, strong, and eager to help out wherever I can on local farms, on the railways, or even in the mine if necessary.' He asked if he could pray before he left. Robert was strangely moved when he saw Tom's absolute stillness as he bowed his head and fervently spoke, *'God of all Grace and Peace, I pray You will give to this family – Eliza, Robert, and Joel, the strength and courage they will need to face whatever lies ahead for them. In Jesus' Name. Amen.'*

CHAPTER FOUR

HEARTACHES

'His temperature's still too high. I've tried everything. I don't know what else to do. I'm scared. He's never been this sick before,' Eliza's frantic cries followed Robert as he mounted Fyre and headed for town.

'I'll ask Doc Armstrong to ride out and see him. He always said he'd come if we had a problem. I'll be as quick as I can. I love you both so very much.'

His mind raced in time with Fyre's pounding hooves. *Judd's been very busy lately. He's been doing a lot of house calls this past winter.* Unusually persistent, soaking rain, with penetrating chill, was replaced by pale warming spring sunshine. It had been a bad season for illness. Talk at the Royal had been full of stories of illnesses and deaths throughout the whole community. Influenza had already claimed many lives in a railway camp several miles north of town.

Reports of seriously ill children circulated with alarming frequency. 'Good to see you,' someone called across the room as Robert pushed through the flap to the Royal Hotel bar.

'I won't be staying long. Had to ask Doc to ride out and check on young Joel. He's been crook for the past few days.'

Sympathetic murmurs mixed with other greetings. Jokes and laughter drew Robert once again into the companionable relaxation the gaggle of men found in the watering hole closeness of the pub.

'You've missed Michael.' Beth smiled at Robert as she slid a beer mug across the bar top. 'He came in earlier looking dreadful. Apparently, Mara's been very ill. She refused to let him bring her into town to see the doc.'

'Her lot would rather be out in the open anyway,' a slurry voice interjected from the back of the room. 'Like all the other abos, the best place for 'em all is back in the bush where they come from.' There was a chorus of boozy agreement. Ribald comments bandied back and forth. 'Useless bastards. Good for nothing! Sons of bitches oughta be shot. Too big a problem,' a belligerent voice from the darkest corner penetrated, clear and offensive.

Robert rose to his feet. Anger at the unfairness of the comment rankled. A red-hot tide rushed up his throat and neck. Many times his friendship with Michael and Mara made him feel like an alien in this place.

'Leave it!' Beth's hand shot out. She grabbed Robert's shoulder. 'It's the booze. Makes 'em experts on a whole range of subjects.'

He settled, but the flush of heat made his face crimson above the beard. His eyes had become two cold, hard brown stones.

For a moment, the lamplight flickered on the diamond on Beth's left hand. 'Heard about that.' He pointed at the ring. 'He's a lucky man.' Grateful for the distraction, he focussed his full attention now on Beth's anxious face.

'Yeah,' piped in another invisible voice in the dark corner. 'Ed's a good bloke. He'll do the right thing by yuh.' Grunts and agreeable mumbles affirmed the fine qualities of Edward Kildark.

Tension in Beth subsided. For a moment, the dimples in her cheeks peeped through the perfectly applied light makeup. She laughed. Her tightly coiled topknot of fair hair bounced buoyantly above the shoulders of her high-necked emerald green top. Her grey green eyes sparkled happily. 'Ah, we've known each other since childhood. We were both born on the road to travelling immigrants – him in Victoria and me in New South Wales. We've got a lot in common. I could only wish his job on the railways didn't keep him away for such a long time.' She laughed again happily. 'Maybe when we're married, I can go with him sometimes. Come on, fellas, fill 'em up again. This one's on the house.'

The noise, chatter, and companionship of shared experiences and stories wrapped around Robert like a blanket. He allowed himself to relax.

'Ten o'clock! Oh my God, poor Eliza!' A casual glance at his pocket watch shocked him. The time had flown. He had been there for two hours.

'Good night,' he called. He pushed his way forcefully through the chattering groups back into the darkness. The sounds and smells followed him as he galloped Fyre back along the riverbank road to home.

The doctor's horse was still tethered to the house gate. It stomped, restless and impatient, in the chilly damp darkness.

A pale moon hung muted silver, its face washed by drifting clouds. The night felt cold and wet, but there was no rain – only soft clinging banks of drifting mist. A gentle wind sighed through the trees and the invisible river in the darkness below murmured an uneasy lullaby.

Robert felt his heart contract with a sudden certainty that something was very wrong.

The hut door opened.

'I'm sorry, Rob.' Dr Judd Armstrong, illuminated by the swinging lantern inside, was a dark, silhouetted shape in the doorway. He was hatless and his hair and beard stood out wild and uncombed. 'There was nothing I could do. Diphtheria is killing all the children. Joel died half an hour ago. His is the sixth death this week. I'm so very, very sorry.'

From inside, Robert heard Eliza's broken sobs. He didn't even see Judd's outstretched hand. He walked with slow, painful heaviness towards the hut and dragged himself up the few steps.

He couldn't speak. He held out his arms. She fell into them. The shuddering pain of inconsolable grief racked their embraced bodies.

Many children died. Day after day, the borough was swamped with news. Shared grieving and even shared funeral services brought some comfort. Each child was a personal tragedy. Everyone coped somehow. Eliza threw herself into furious activity. She was often up and gone before Robert woke. He never asked what she was doing in the far paddocks. He knew she dug, weeded, and repaired fences. There was nothing requiring such frantic activity. He respected her need to keep busy. He found it hard to care. *Getting out of bed is my biggest challenge.*

'You couldn't even come home when your son was dying,' she had screamed at him. 'You weren't even here to say goodbye. Drinks with the fellas have always been more important than we ever were. Go on then, Robert, spend your life boozing. I no longer care.'

'I'm sorry, Liza. I looked for Judd all over town, and when I found him I only dropped into the Royal, intending to stay a few minutes. I... I ... oh, love, can't we sit and talk about this? I can't turn the clock back. We need to be helping each other.'

She knew she was being unfair, but a cold, dead feeling inside made nothing matter anyway. The anger was replaced by an inability to speak, and she'd simply moved away.

This set a pattern. She now moved around the hut like a pale silent ghost. With drooping shoulders and no spark of fire or feeling, she automatically did what she had to do. Their small crops flourished. She didn't care and he didn't notice.

In silence, days passed and they, each in their own way, functioned.

In the first week, Robert had tried. 'I'll do anything – anything at all to make this easier for you.'

'Nothing will make this easier,' she had snarled. 'I don't care what you do. I'll be OK. I simply don't care.'

'I'd like to get a job on the railways,' he announced one morning during breakfast. The silence between them felt particularly oppressive. 'I can see a big future here when the line comes through.'

Eliza looked across the table at him. Her heavy mane of brown hair fell loosely around her shoulders. Her white face was set and still. She simply nodded. Her gaze was devoid of all questioning or interest.

'I believe they're recruiting in town this week.' She nodded again.

He reached out and touched her hand. 'Love, I know we're going to get through this. I want to do what's best for us both. I'm hoping for a job that will give us a more secure income. I'll try to get one close to town in administration, so I will rarely be away from home.'

'Rob!' The sound of her voice resonated shrilly. 'I really don't care. I came here to be with you and Joel. I didn't really want to come. Now Joel's gone, I don't think I'd be happy anywhere. I'm here now. This is where I'll stay, and you can do whatever you like whenever you want to.' The brittle sharpness of her reply pierced him, but he detected a quiver of brokenness.

The warmth of love they once knew was still there somewhere. For now, it had disappeared among the hurt and pain.

He shivered.

'I'll start digging up the potatoes in the river paddock,' he said. He pushed himself to make an effort as he grabbed his hat and moved towards the door. 'They're probably ready now for marketing. Love, things will get better. I know they will. Please give it time.' He moved to gather her into his arms. She cringed back into her chair.

As Eliza collected up the cutlery, cups, and plates and placed them carefully in the basin of hot soapy water, he made his way slowly and sadly out into the already warm spring sunshine.

She didn't look up.

He only got as far as the back paddock before he sat down on a tree stump, clutching Joel's yellow bucket. He'd picked it up when he had stopped at the shed. It had been forgotten beside the spade in the corner.

'I don't think I can bear this,' he cried out to the cloudless, unhearing blue sky. 'Joel was my little mate. He's only one of many who've died these past weeks, but he was my little boy and life will never be the same.'

Acute pain of loss and sorrow knifed through his body. As he groaned, a refrain of infinite longing poured from his heart. 'It's now we need each other the most. Help me. Please help me! We need each other. Help me. Please help me!'

He bowed his head and sobbed heart-wrenching gasps of total despair.

His eyes looked back at the hut. 'Eliza,' he said softly, 'this is grief we should be sharing.' A desperate longing for the warmth of her embrace washed over him.

'Liza! Liza!' His voice was caught and held by the wind. It sighed through the trees.

Inside the hut, Liza thought she heard a cry. It pierced through the crippling pain of her own sorrow. She too cried. 'Oh, Rob, will we ever find our way back?'

For a moment in the desire to comfort him, she felt the first stirrings of hope.

Rob, Rob, can we find the way back to each other?

CHAPTER FIVE

MICHAEL – GRIEF AND LEGACY

MICHAEL LOOKED BACK at the tent, grey and indistinct now in the distance. The midnight moonless darkness enveloped its shape with fingers of shadow. The river was a wide black ribbon of gentle whispering movement.

He wrapped his arms more tightly around the lifeless body of his wife. He stumbled on. The spade hit the top of his boots as he walked. He didn't even feel the thud as it connected with his knees.

His face was wet with tears. His breathing, laboured by sobs, forced its way through trembling lips. 'Mara, Mara! I can't believe you've gone.'

She was already dead when he came home. Curled up, she looked peaceful but cold in her bedroll. Influenza had hit her hard. Even when she seemed to be recovering, she had looked frail and ill. Her death shocked him. It wasn't totally unexpected. Reports of deaths from influenza and diphtheria continued to climb in the whole colony. This was Mara and the pain of her loss pierced him to the core of his being.

They laughed when I wanted to marry you. Gins are for the taking, some drunks bawled out from an alley one night. Michael shuddered at the memory. He knew he was capable of murder at that time. *No one knew back then or even understands today that I truly love you. You are my wife – a part of me. I've always been so proud. Proud of your courage. Proud of your dignity.*

'Mara! Mara, me darlin', life will certainly be the poorer witout yuh!'

He held her tenderly and close until he reached the fork in the river. Now he headed into the gully beside the branched-off creek. Gently, he placed her body on the grassy bank and began to dig.

'I don't care if the authorities think you should be buried in their new cemetery. Here is where you said you wanted. Here is where 'tis goin' to be! Chances are they couldn't care less,' he muttered as he carefully flattened the soil over the deep hole containing her body. 'You're not even counted as a citizen anyway.'

Michael shivered as he made his slow way back to the campsite. Grief surged through his body like a physical pain. How was he ever going to tell the child? Was she prepared? He had left her sleeping peacefully. He thought he would spare her suffering by removing her mother's body, but now he wondered if he'd done the right thing.

He sat on his bedroll in the darkness and rocked gently back and forth, arms folded, his body racked by grieving sorrow. 'Oh, Mara, Mara, me luv,' he moaned.

He didn't hear the child wake. Suddenly, she was there beside him. Her hands stroked his beard and her golden eyes looked up with compassion into his brown ones. 'Daddy' was all she said. The wisdom of the ages was in her expression and the pain of inconsolable loss in her voice. With only the briefest glance at her mother's empty bedroll, Nika climbed on to her father's lap. She buried her tear-stained face into the comfort of his shoulder.

There they sat and sorrowed, locked in a tight embrace. The night slowly lost its black intensity and the first light of dawn touched the distant hills with gold.

Somewhere out in the hidden distance, Michael sensed rather than heard a keening sound of grieving. *Her people would know,* he thought. *In that knowing way of theirs, they would know that Marrangaroo... their little blue flowers is no longer with us.*

'Wherever now your spirit journeys, me luv, may you find your peace.'

'They … they call me "nigger".' Nika felt the words forced from her mouth. She desperately wanted to remain silent, but Michael's cold insistence broke through her resistance. He had found her huddled, crying in the corner of the tent. He cradled her gently and kissed the tears from her cheek. She could feel the fierce violence of his anger shuddering through the thin material of her cotton dress.

'They say Abo children shouldn't even be at school.' The whole truth was only part of the story she hesitantly sobbed out. She was frightened of his anger and fearful of what he might do.

She had been at the school for only a few weeks. In the beginning, determined to ignore the opposition she sensed from all sides, she had kept to herself. Some of the children had been openly violent – a shove here, a push there, the foot that seemed to come from nowhere and left her sprawling in the red dust. Dust in powdery profusion covered the entire flat square of the assembly area in front of the schoolhouse. (This two-roomed structure had been proudly built by local farmers with timber donated by the forestry company.)

Even many of the adults had been hostile. Parents and the teacher talked in penetrating whispers. Their words and snickers made her feel as if she was invisible. 'I didn't know that Aboriginal children were going to be allowed in the school,' one of them called across the heads of the assembled children. 'Just because her father's white doesn't alter anything. Education and these limited facilities were to be for *our* children.'

Nika had learnt well the lessons of quiet stillness from her mother. Most times, she covered her ears, concentrated on the birds wheeling overhead, and watched the kangaroos gathering under the shade trees. Her eyes focussed and strained to catch a glimpse of the river in the distance.

She loved school. Words painted pictures in her mind and she loved nothing better than to transcribe every letter she saw on to her slate.

It became a living instrument and the forming words journeyed through her mind. It made sense so quickly she liked to write down everything she read. She even wrote in the dirt as she sounded out the letters for the things around her. Carefully, she wrote 'gate,' 'fence,' 'dirt,' 'bird,' 'sky', and 'water' and spoke them triumphantly into the atmosphere.

The day Billy Jenkins deliberately scuffed his feet through the neat pattern of her writing and laughed as he watched the spiralling wind take all her words away was a day Nika would never forget.

It was such a silly, simple thing, but for a brief moment she broke out of her gentle stillness and grabbed a handful of his dirty, matted blond hair and shook him. It was a sharp, brief shake, but in her heart she wished she could have held on and shaken him till she wiped the stupid, triumphant smirk from his dirty face. The incident was over quickly, but the repercussions had gone on for days.

'You can't trust these abos!' Matt Jenkins, holding the hand of his grinning offspring, had returned the next morning. As he stomped up the half a dozen timber steps to the narrow veranda of the schoolhouse, he'd yelled for all to hear. 'Time we did something about this! School's was not built for them abos! They don't need no educatin'!' Send 'em all back to the bush where they belong! I was sayin' to the missus only yesterday they'd be happier in the bush where they belong. What's the use of educatin' 'em? Yuh don't need no schoolin' ta work in a homestead kitchen or herd a few cows. They're blimmin' useless at mining. The school was built for our kids. I really don't think we should be taking in any Abo ones.'

'Nika has been here for several weeks now,' a gentle female voice interjected. 'As far as I know, she's not caused any trouble.'

'Can't trust 'em,' Matt muttered again. 'Yuh think they're gentle people when suddenly they want to kill yuh. No, I reckon we're on a dangerous course here. Let one in for schoolin', the next thing yuh know you'll be flooded with 'em and there won't be enough places for our own kids. The borough is growing all the time.

'After all, the Government said free schoolin' for all the kids, but that's not countin' the Abo ones – free schoolin' for all the kids of the townsfolk. I reckon Michael should be asked to take Nika away.'

'Perhaps he could teach her himself,' someone else interjected.

Nika told her father none of these things but simply added, 'They don't think I should be at the school, Dad.'

'We'll see about that.' Michael was already whistling for his horse as he stomped across the paddock, dragging her behind him. She ran to keep up with his long strides.

The black stallion came at his summons and waited patiently as he was saddled. He snorted eagerly as the man and child settled themselves on his strong back.

'I wonder why they're up there looking at us,' Nika suddenly exclaimed, pointing across the river. Michael wheeled the horse and peered in the direction of the broken rocky escarpment ridge. Even in the fading light of the late afternoon and the shadows cast by the background line of green tree-covered hills, Michael could see two horsemen.

They disappeared as he watched, but he felt a prickle of uncertainty. A chill for a second touched his mind.

'Ah, 'tis probably only some wandering miners,' he said, laughing down at the child. He hugged her closer to his chest as he urged the horse into a canter.

Miss Frances Phillips patted nervously at the tight coiled plait of her auburn hair. The severe starched collar on her high-necked grey dress rustled as she settled herself more comfortably at the table. It was piled with papers. The breeze through the wooden slatted window rustled the edges of the loose sheets. She moved a pile of slates to one side and smiled nervously as Michael loomed in the doorway.

His face looked flushed and angry. His luxurious black beard overflowed his shirt front and a tangle of bright curls fell on to his forehead. There was something in the dark eyes that arrested her attention. She saw a desperate mute appeal there and a vulnerable softness around his mouth.

'Please sit down, Mr O'Reilly.'

Michael compressed his large frame into the confines of the narrow straight-backed timber chair. His eyes connected with hers.

'Please,' he said, 'it's important Nika gets a good education. Life will be difficult enough for her. She needs to be educated.'

He pushed a small parcel across the table.

'Look, I'm not expecting free schooling for Nika. I'm asking only that she be given a chance. I've had this assessed.' He patted the parcel. 'It's worth a great deal of money. I'm willing to give it to the education authorities in exchange for her schooling.'

Frances poked a tentative finger at the hard round parcel and it slowly unwrapped. At first glance, it looked like a piece of pitted rock, but she suddenly saw a flash of colour in the light. 'It's a gold nugget,' she gasped. 'It's real gold. Where did you get it?' Warily suspicious, she pushed the object back across the table.

'It's mine. I've told the mining bods. My claim down the river came good. You can pass it on to the school board. Cash it in – use it for the future of the school, but you must sign an agreement with me that Nika will receive the maximum amount of schooling that this borough can provide.'

'I … I don't know whether they can agree to that, Michael. I'll certainly tell them of your offer, but policy is policy. I don't think there can be any exceptions.'

Michael rose to his feet. 'Keep it,' he said, pushing the nugget back across the rough timber surface of the table. 'Show it to them. Let them see how much good it can do your school and let Nika know your decision. She'll be here as usual in the mornin'.'

He turned at the door, his voice appealing, face desperate. 'Please,' he said, 'do what you can. She deserves a chance.'

He strode down the steps, walked across the hard square of dusty, baked dirt assembly area, and waved to Nika. She was under the trees at the bottom of the schoolyard, writing something in the dirt with a stick. 'Time to go, me darlin',' he called cheerfully. 'We'd best be tinkin' about our dinner.'

Frances watched them ride away. She reached for the nugget. It was very heavy in her hand. 'Real gold! Wow! It must be worth a fortune. I hope something can be arranged to help Nika. I'll certainly do the best I can.'

CHAPTER SIX

TRAGEDIES – NEW BEGINNINGS

Unexpectedly, the hot afternoon silence was splintered by the sound of galloping horses crossing the open river plain. A rifle shot cracked. The moment of unnatural, suspended calm was followed by a second and then a third shot. They whistled, hummed, and thudded into their target.

Loud male voices – belligerent and crude – mouthed obscenities as footsteps pounded now across the campsite. The boiling billy fell as a booted foot slammed into the supporting timber frame. It sloshed, hissing into the heart of the log-fire's heat.

'This is life or death.' Terrified, Nika cringed at the back of the tent. Through the narrow open flap, she could see her father's body. It was an unnaturally twisted mound hunched only inches from the pawing hooves of his terrified stallion. She knew he was dead. The ground surrounding him was a glistening pool of red.

Two men struggled to remove the saddlebags from the horse's back. The big black's panic made the task difficult. He bucked and weaved, flinging their bodies to and fro. Suddenly, with a final desperate yank, a strap broke. The bag jerked free. The men fell to the ground in a tangle of waving arms and legs. Sunlight caught the glint of scattered golden nuggets.

Nika's control broke. 'Daddy! Daddy!' she screamed.

Startled, the two men turned. 'Bloody hell,' one shouted, 'his kid's there. She's probably seen our faces.'

Frozen, Nika watched them stride towards the tent.

She couldn't run. Her legs shook uncontrollably. Gasping for breath as her heart pounded mercilessly against her ribs, she willed herself to unwind from the tight ball her body had formed in the corner. She felt like she was pinned to the ground.

Then a large man's hand reached out to grab her. Her eyes fixed in horror at dirt-ingrained fingers and little tufts of matted dusty hair growing below the knotted knuckles.

Again she screamed. In that moment, tension broke and her body once more came to life. Ducking as the hand grabbed for her hair, she ran as the second man lunged in her direction.

Distraught, she ran in weaving drunken panic for the bushes. She looked back at her father. The horse, now still, nuzzled hot breaths across his lifeless body.

Nika continued running. Sheer terror spurred her on. Her heart felt like it would burst. Still, the footsteps pounded after her. She realised, with shock, the jarring sound in her ears was the sound of her own voice. Nika screamed as she ran, but she knew she was too far away for anyone to help her.

Forcing herself to steady the panic, she stopped and stripped off her brightly coloured dress. She flung it as far as she could, then turned sharply and plunged into the deeper bush.

This was familiar country to her. She had played here often, hiding and making trails to find her way out again. When she was too exhausted to run any further, she pushed through even deeper scrub and then dropped on to the floor of a small cave, at the base of a high rock escarpment.

The sound of her gasping, sobbing breaths reverberated around the chamber. Her thin body, naked except for the white V of her pants, was scratched and bleeding. Insect bites covered her feet and legs with red weals. With her hand over her mouth, she struggled to calm her breathing and listened intently. There was no sound now of following footsteps.

The child fell into an exhausted sleep in the quiet stillness.

Shadows lengthened until the thick impenetrable blanket of darkness dropped. The bush settled into a deep, profound slumber. Possum eyes flickered red–orange lights. Other nocturnal creatures moved silently through the trees and along the rough surface of the ground.

Nika dreamed that night of her mother. Marrangaroo, wafting dark as the surrounding night yet radiant with an inner light, gently caressed her grieving, battered body. She sat beside her and stroked her hair. She held her tenderly, soothed her, and spoke peace into her mind.

'Go to town, my child, my darling one. Don't stay in the bush. Go to town. Keep up with your schooling. Your future is still a bright one. You are loved. You will be loved *forever*.'

The stench of beer and spirits filled the alley between the clustered buildings. It was obviously drifting from the hotels further down the street.

The alley was dark and damp. Afternoon showers had disappeared, but the ground dust and the walls of the buildings were sticky with a cloying mouldy odour.

Robert wove a slow way towards the stables behind the hardware store. He'd been drinking but was still sober and knew he should go home early tonight. *While things at home are still not good, I'll try to make them better.*

Fyre must have recognised his footsteps. The stomping neigh of welcome pierced through the sounds of distant laughter and bawdy conversation.

He didn't see the huddled form curled up in the darkness. He would have tripped if he hadn't used his hand to steady himself.

The shape beneath his grasp suddenly shuddered into a human sitting position. A child's voice whimpered, 'Go away. Go away! Take your hand off me.'

Robert peered into the dirty, tear-stained face of a sobbing child. A thin shaft of moonlight for a moment touched the featureless bundle of clothing. A strand of yellow-gold hair shone in the light.

'Nika? Nika, is that you? My God! This is no place for you to be sleeping.'

Anger against Mike burnt fiercely. *You drunken sod! Ruin your own life if you must, but surely your kid deserves a chance.*

Nika struggled furiously. She knew she had gone to sleep in a dangerous place. The brothel was only around the corner. She really hadn't any idea where else to go. 'Don't touch me!' she cried again, cringing back against the wall and hitting at him with her fists.

'Nika, it's Robert Barritt.' He bent down and spoke gently and carefully, 'Nika, I'm not going to hurt you. You remember me, don't you? I want to help you. Where's your father?'

Struggling frantically, she lurched to her feet. She would have fled down the alley, but he caught her hand. 'Nika, you can't go out there. It's not safe. A lot of the men are already blind drunk. Where's your father?'

'He's dead! He's dead!' Now she screamed hysterically, 'Men came and killed him. They stole the gold. He … he had some in his saddlebags. I saw it fall out on to the ground.

'They shot him! He's dead. I didn't know what to do. They tried to catch me. I kept running and running. I don't know where they are now.

I don't know what to do. I got away. I slept in a cave. Daddy's body is still at the campsite. I couldn't help him. I just ran. Oh … oh… I … I don't know what I'm going to do now.' She began to rock back and forth, moaning, 'I … I don't know where to go. My father is dead! Now my mother and my father are both dead. All our stuff – all we've ever owned was by the river. The horses have gone. The tent and our stuff should be still there, but maybe, maybe they came back and took it all.' Her whole body shook with violent sobbing as her hands pounded desperately into his chest.

Robert put his arms around her. All he could do was hold her tightly. His mind was in turmoil. He prayed no one else would come until he worked out what he was going to do.

He didn't feel he had a choice. He had to take her home with him. Eliza had hardly spoken to him for weeks now. They lived quiet but completely separate lives. *How will she handle this – a child suddenly thrust upon her?* Thoughts chased in spiralling circles in his mind as Nika's gulping sobs gradually subsided into gasps. Finally, she lay quietly against his chest. 'Come on,' he said gently into her hair. 'We'll go home now. I'll fix up everything else in the morning.'

'I … I went back,' she sobbed. 'I … I'd lost my dress and I grabbed some things out of the tent …, but … but I … I can't find the horses and I … I … covered Daddy with a blanket and lots of our stuff seems to be missing and I … I … then I walked to town. I've been walking for hours. I don't know what else to do.' Her sobs intensified into choking gasps. Her frail body trembled in Robert's arms.

'Come on, love,' he said again tenderly. He stroked her hair. 'We'll sort it all out in the morning. Let's go home now.'

Fyre saw them emerge from the alley and snickered a delighted welcome. He stood patiently as Robert saddled up and settled the child in front. Her pathetic bundle of possessions was now tied to a saddle strap. It bounced against Robert's leg as he rode. His head was full of questions as they cantered along the river path leading to the hut.

Michael must have been killed late yesterday. Nika must have spent last night in the cave. The trail will already be cold. They must have taken the horses. But Michael's stallion is too distinctive. They couldn't be seen with it. They'd have to get rid of it very quickly. Mara's mare would be easier to hide, but she's older and slower. How long was the child alone at the campsite with her father's body? How soon can I get back to bury him? How is Eliza going to handle this? Oh poor Michael! What an awful way for it all to end!

His head throbbed with the confused mixture of questions, grief, and uncertainty.

He carried Nika as he dismounted and removed the chain from the top gate. Surprised, he saw a thin flicker of candlelight inside the hut below. He focussed on it as he gently guided Fyre down the path to home. *Eliza must be still up.*

Eliza heard Fyre's appreciative whinny as he was released into the paddock. She walked towards the door. Robert was home earlier tonight and she was determined there would be some communication between them. They were like strangers and she knew the fault was hers. She'd have to do something to make amends. Perhaps welcoming him home would be a starting point.

He stood in the doorway. The weight of the child's sleeping body in his arms caused him to sway. The flickering candle played on his face, highlighting lines of tiredness around his eyes. Nika moaned and stirred restlessly. Her hair fell forward in a tumbling mass.

'Nika!' The shocked stillness that had settled on Eliza when she saw a child in Robert's arms broke. 'Nika! What's happened, Robert? What's the girl doing here?'

'I don't know much at this stage. But … but Nika tells me both Marrangaroo and Michael are dead. Liza, I … I … didn't know what else to do. I found Nika in the alley. All I could think about was bringing her home to you.'

Eliza sighed. 'Of course, she can stay the night here. But … but, Robert, I … I … don't really know if I can bear to have another child in this hut with us.'

He reached across and gently placed an arm around her shoulders. 'Dear, all we can do for now is put Nika to bed and let tomorrow sort itself out. I'm so sorry, love, to have put this on you. I really didn't have a choice.'

She moved to share the weight of the sleeping girl in his arms. He was touched when he saw the flicker of tenderness lighten the sternness of her expression. 'You poor, poor child,' she crooned as she gently rocked her back and forth.

He knew it had been a long time since his wife had displayed any emotion in his presence. He tenderly kissed her forehead. 'Do you need anything?'

'No, I can make up the trundle bed for her. All the linens on the shelf.' She disappeared into the back room with a gentle caress of sleeping Nika's arm and a smile in his direction.

'Why did you need the candle?'

'Out of kerosene,' she called back from the darkness.

When Robert heard Nika suddenly cry out, he was reassured when he heard the tenderness of Eliza's reply. 'Shh, Nika, love.

Everything's going to be all right. You're safe with us. No one's going to hurt you. No one's going to take you away from us.'

VALE MICHAEL – LEGACY

It WAS THE hardest morning of Robert's life. He thought the death of Joel would never be surpassed for feelings of helplessness and inadequacy. Standing at the river's edge, looking down at Michael's covered body, those feelings were intensified, and he was overwhelmed by a mind-numbing anger.

'The rotten bastards!' His eyes swept the desecrated campsite.

There was no sign of the horses and Michael's few possessions had been strewn around, clothing and foodstuffs mixed in jumbled confusion. It was as if a whirlwind had blown in from the hills. Obviously, the search had been frantic. The lure for gold once more had made animals out of human greed. The ground was stomped and battered. Even the tent had been slashed in a display of frustrated anger. *I don't know how Nika ever got away or how she had the courage to come back again.*

'Mike, I'm sorry. I'm so sorry. I wish with all my heart there was something I could have done.' He looked down at the covered body. Nika had done her best to tuck the blanket around her father's shoulders. Robert was shocked to see that someone had even stripped the corpse, searching pockets and boots for hidden treasure. Again, his thoughts went to the child. *Nika, what a nightmare this has been for you.*

'I give you my word, mate.' He kneeled beside the lifeless body. 'I'll look after your girl. I'll do everything to see she wants for nothing and… and … we *will* find who did this. One day, my friend, justice will be done.'

The police knew he was riding out to the campsite at first light. 'I told Constable Bart I'd leave everything as I found it and touch nothing. I hate leaving you like this, Mike, but I know he'll be here before too long. There was a riot at the mine last night. He's got a few things to sort out on the way. Goodbye, my friend. Glad to have known you, for even such a short time.'

Michael was buried in the new cemetery. This cemetery replaced the early miners' cleared internment area, which mainly consisted of unmarked, scattered mounds.

He would probably have preferred an unmarked grave by the river beside Mara. He didn't really have a choice and the authorities felt an official burial site was more appropriate after the indignities of his murder. He was surrounded by plenty of company in his final resting place. The open paddock was pockmarked with covered mounds. Many small diphtheria victims were also buried here. Most graves had no markers, but a few of the larger ones had an added note carved beneath their names on simple wooden crosses: 'Victim of Influenza, 1881'.

A few of the graves had more permanent headstones. A stone mason had only recently arrived in town. Michael was buried in the plot beside Joel.

Nika was pleased her father's grave would be clearly marked. She kneeled and placed a flower on the mound of freshly dug earth,

Frances Phillips, an anonymous black shape with a disguising dark veil, separated herself from the large group of mourners. 'Robert, Eliza! Could I please speak with you for a moment?'

Eliza and Rob turned. They didn't recognise the figure but moved towards her. Nika still kneeled beside the grave. Tears stained the brown clay soil as she grieved.

'I … I wanted to catch up with you.' Frances gently steered them to the edge of the moving crowd. Her voice was soft – little more than a whisper.

Robert smiled, his eyes questioning.

'It … it's about Nika. I … don't know what you're planning to do, but I … I felt you should know. I … I'm her teacher by the way. Frances Phillips. ' Robert moved closer and shook her hand. They both smiled. Frances spoke rapidly and softly as if she needed to get the words out before being overheard. 'The education authorities have accepted Michael's offer, providing it's not made general knowledge. Nika will be able to attend school for as long as she desires. The agreement stipulates she is to be given every opportunity and there is no cut-off time indicated.'

'I heard something about Mike's plan for Nika's education. My God, his nugget must have been worth a fortune to influence the Government in this way! I'll do my best to see she continues at school. She's been taught to ride and I can come as far as town with her most days. The school is only another mile down the road. I … oh, leave it with me anyway. I'll make sure she can get to school.'

Suddenly, Eliza's soft voice interjected. 'Rob, we have a lot to talk about, but … but do you think we could legally adopt Nika?'

Robert directed a surprised glance in her direction and gently reached out and squeezed her hand. 'I believe it's what Mara and Mike would have wanted,' she continued gently.

'This whole business is most unusual,' Frances called back as she disappeared into the crowd. 'Mike certainly opened the door for his daughter. I'm glad he signed all the legal documents before he died. They certainly have to honour them now. I'm pleased for Nika – very pleased. She's a good student.'

They ambled slowly home in the dray later that day… . Nika's shy voice suddenly broke the silence. 'Rob, where did they find my … my mother's horse?'

'She was running free by the river a few miles south of your campsite. Constable Bart thinks they let her go because she was slowing them down.'

'I don't think Tige will be going with them willingly either,' Nika added sadly. 'He wouldn't have wanted to leave Daddy's body.'

'Tige.' Robert smiled gently back at her. 'I didn't even know that huge black stallion of your father's had a name. From what I've seen of him, he'll be a handful.'

'Oh, Tige looks big and fearsome, but he's as gentle as can be if you *love* him.' Silent tears once more slid down her cheeks.

Eliza moved across the wooden seat and gathered the child's thin body in her arms. 'We'll get him back, love. We'll bring him home to us. Maybe you'll be able to ride him. And one day, they'll find the men who killed your dad. Constable Bart says he and his friend Jake will never give up looking.'

Robert let the reins slacken in his hands and the horse slowed down, ambling gently now towards the home paddock. He didn't turn around. 'Nika, I … know this is a bit soon, but I want you to really think about something.

'Liza and I would like to officially make you our daughter. We know we're more of an age to be your elder brother and sister, but we want to make you officially part of our family.

'We need to do this quickly in case someone wants to take you to the local authorities or send you to an orphanage in the city. They wouldn't give you to your mother's people. We really want to do what's best for you. We believe Mara and Mike would want us to care for you. How do you feel? I know, dear, it's all a bit soon, but we have to make the decisions now.'

'I would like to stay with you.' The girl's voice was choked with tears. 'Would I have to be called Nika Barritt?'

'Oh, Nika,' Eliza interrupted happily. 'We want you to really be in our family. We'll be proud to call you our child.'

'I'm sorry, so sorry.' Nika cried, sobbing hysterically. 'I'm Nika O'Reilly. I really don't want to be anyone else. I'm Nika O'Reilly! Please, please don't make me change.'

'Whoa!' Robert halted the dray and turned to give his full attention to the woman and girl in the back seat.

Eliza sat in rigid straight-backed serenity. Her face was animated, alive like it hadn't been since Joel's death. 'We'll love you, Nika, and always treat you as our own.'

Robert reached and gently squeezed Nika's shoulder. 'I don't understand the law, but I'll see what can be worked out.' He smiled compassionately at the grieving child. 'I think we can legally adopt you as Nika O'Reilly and you could be called Nika O'Reilly Barritt. Would that be better?'

She continued to sob, but her eyes looked up at him. Slowly and sadly, she nodded. Eliza gathered her more tightly to her side. Robert flicked the reins and the horse moved on again. Gradually, the rhythmic sway of the dray's movements washed over them. The tension in Nika's frail body relaxed and she fell into a deep sleep, her head pillowed in Eliza's lap.

Robert glanced at his wife. Between them flashed the shared connectedness of understanding, grief, and compassion. They both knew with profound certainty that a new chapter in their lives had just begun.

CHAPTER EIGHT

RENEWED CONNECTION

'THAT MUST BE Tom's horse,' Eliza's voice broke the silence. For the last two miles, she had dozed, her head resting on Nika's shoulder, the exhausted child's sleeping body draped across her knee. A brown mare galloped past as Robert brought the dray to a creaking halt. He jumped down to open the top gate.

The horse nuzzled his hand. 'It looks like her. I don't know any other horse with a white blaze behind the ear like this one.' He fondled her ears affectionately. She galloped away, contented.

'Hi, folks!' Tom's blurred shape sharpened into clear focus as he sprang up at their approach. 'I was resting on your veranda. I've been riding since sunup.' His face as usual was clean-shaven but coated with

48

dust. His hair was a tousled cap of disarray. He looked tired – his green eyes penetrating but clouded. Even his wide friendly grin drooped at the edges.

'Come in. I'll make us all a cup of tea,' Eliza called cheerfully. Robert assisted her out of the dray and together they carried the child to the lounge room. The girl sank into the depths of the large armchair still fast asleep.

'I'll put the dray in the shed. I'll only be a few minutes. That cup of tea sounds great.' Robert smiled as he disappeared outside.

'How are you, Liza?' Tom's concerned voice mingled with the crackling of wood. He stood behind her watching as she kneeled and rekindled the flames by blowing on the embers.

'I think I'm getting there. What you said about God having a purpose for all our lives made sense to me. All I can do is take one day at a time and trust Him for the strength to live it. How's everything going with you, Tom?'

He didn't answer immediately. His attention was distracted as the child suddenly moved in the chair. Through the doorway, he could see her. 'Oh, I'm OK, but I've been in the saddle a lot lately.'

'Tom, that's Nika, Michael's daughter. I don't suppose you've met her before.'

'No, I haven't. She's quite startling, isn't she? A bit of a shock when you see her for the first time.'

Nika lay with knees drawn up, her dark green dress covering all but the tips of her brown shoes. Her face was at peace now and settled in the soft lines of childhood. Her delicately arched black eyebrows gave expression even to her sleeping face. Her skin glowed with a healthy copper sheen, and as her hair caught the fire glow, it splayed across the chair back in tendrils of living light.

'She's lovely – very lovely,' Tom sighed. 'She'll have to be guarded well in this rough place.'

Robert walked in. 'I suppose you heard about Michael?'

'Yes, that's one of the reasons I rode here before heading north to Maryborough. I heard in town the funeral was today.'

'That's where we've been. A difficult, very sad, but necessary morning.' Robert sighed deeply. He lowered himself into a chair. His body felt heavy and tired. A knot of grief still compacted his chest. 'Here, Tom,' he said quietly, 'come and sit by the window. The kettle's almost boiled.'

'Is there anything I can do about Michael?' Tom whispered. Robert suspected he was trying not to wake the child. 'I … I heard he was murdered. The story they've been circulating down the line is that Mara's dead too. Influenza I was told. There's been so much tragedy in these last few months.' His voice faltered. 'Every single day has brought news of something else.'

'Mara apparently died only a few weeks before Mike's diggings came good, and according to all the stories we've heard, Michael became a bit of a recluse. He told no one and we didn't see him much in town at all. Then we heard he'd struck it rich. Some of the nuggets are already in circulation. Mike wasted no time in verifying his claim and fixing up all the legal stuff.'

'We were told today he's even arranged for Nika's schooling.' Eliza began pouring tea into the lined up mugs on the table. 'Help yourselves. Biscuits are in the tin there. Rob, will you please grab the milk from the cooling chest?'

Robert moved across to where the net-covered, light-framed box was suspended from a hook in the ceiling. He passed her a small jug. 'We're so grateful for daily fresh milk from our neighbour's cow.' He sat down again beside Tom.

Tom's eyes continued to drift to the sleeping child in the chair. 'Is there anything I can do about her? There are a few church agencies, particularly in Brisbane. They operate homes for displaced children and adults. I would certainly try to find the best one.'

'We're going to adopt her,' Robert interrupted. His voice sounded sharper than he intended. 'As soon as I can get to the solicitor in town, I'll begin the process.'

'No one's going to take her from us.' Eliza's vehemence shocked Tom. Her face was radiant. He'd hate to see her disappointed. Then a sudden thought relaxed his anxiety. *She'd still be considered an*

Aboriginal by the census folk. Officially, she doesn't exist. Don't think anyone's going to care much about her case.

'If this is what you really want, we'll pray together later that everything goes smoothly.' He didn't share with them his own feelings that probably no one would care if she simply 'disappeared'. He smiled across at them. 'I believe the purposes of God are beyond our understanding. Maybe indeed Nika's life is meant to be joined with yours.'

'We'll love her.' Eliza added, 'Tom, have no doubt that if she lives permanently with us, it will be as a member of our family, not as a servant or a ward. I want her to know this from the beginning. We're not just "taking her in" out of charity. She will be our child.'

Forgive me, Father. Tom's silent prayer was from his heart. *I thought it was an act of Christian duty. They really love her. Bless this family. Help the legalities to flow smoothly. Amen.*

'I believe you're working for the railways now, Rob. Some of the talk round town is that you've got some sort of administration work connected with the planning for the new line.'

'Oh, nothing very important or special,' Robert laughed. 'I lined up when they were recruiting, and instead of sending me out in the hot sun, they decided I should spend most of my time in a little office at the back of the proposed rail storage shed. I keep all the diagrams and updates on the progress of the line. Occasionally, I ride out and see how it's going. Reckon we'll be celebrating the line's opening, 'bout the middle of next year.'

He laughed again, but his eyes still retained their expression of tired sadness. 'Keeps me out of mischief, gives me a bit of extra income, although there's still plenty to do around here. We make enough to keep us goin'. I know we've got a lot to be thankful for.'

Nika suddenly stirred. Uncertain of her new surroundings, she let out a frightened cry. Eliza immediately ran to her. 'Shh, it's OK, love. You're quite safe. You're here at home with Rob and Eliza.'

With her arm protectively across the girl's shoulder, they returned together to the table. 'Here you go, Nika. Sit here next to Tom. Would you like some milk and a biscuit?'

Nika sat where Eliza directed and looked up at the stranger perched awkwardly on the chair next to her. He had a nice face. She looked up at him shyly.

'Tom, this is Nika. Nika, Tom Daniels.' Robert smiled across the table.

'Oh, I've heard about you. My dad said you're one of the folks that ride everywhere telling people about God.'

'Well, yes.' He laughed. 'I'm surprised myself to find there are a few of us from different denominations. I believe with all my heart the future of this community depends upon its roots being founded on godly principles. Jesus Christ needs to be the anchor for the human souls. Oops, sorry. Didn't mean to preach. Pleased to meet you!'

He smiled. Politely and seriously, he shook the girl's hand. 'How old are you, Nika? I have it in my mind Michael once told me you were almost eleven.'

'I've turned eleven now,' she answered shyly. 'My birthday is in September – in the springtime. This year my mum died in the same week.' Her voice trailed off. Tom admired her courage as she struggled to stop the tears from flowing by putting her hands up to her eyes and clenching her teeth.

Instinctively, he reached out and hugged her to his side. She looked up at him. Her eyes for a moment studied his face and then she smiled – a beautiful smile tinged with sadness. Her dark eyes glistened with unshed tears. They flashed with golden lights. Something deep inside him jumped. His chest contracted. He could hardly breathe. *Oh God, she's lovely.*

I like him, Nika thought. *He's a kind person.*

Tom's visit only lasted a couple of hours, but he was rested when he saddled up and prepared for departure.

'I'll call and see how you're doing when I'm back this way. Probably in a month or two.' He waved and had turned the horse to canter away when a voice shouted from the top gate. It caused him to rein in sharply in order to hear more clearly.

'Tom Daniels?' the voice yelled. 'Is Tom Daniels still here?'

'That's our neighbour's son, Layton,' Robert remarked to Eliza. 'I wonder what he wants.'

Tom called back. 'Yes, I'm here. I'll come up to you. Bye, folks. Bye, Nika. See you all soon.' He urged the horse onwards and cantered up the hill to the gate.

'I thought I saw you ride past earlier,' the voice from the distance still yelled. 'We've had word there's been an accident at the rail siding – the Maryborough side – at Slater's Creek. If you're riding that way, could you check? A few of the men have been hurt. I know help will come from further north, but if you're heading that way, there may be something you can do.'

'I'm heading that way. Ride with me to your boundary fence and tell me what you know.'

Tom turned and waved again at the three figures on the hut veranda as he refastened the top gate. The two horses and riders disappeared through the trees. The fading sound of galloping hooves disturbed the silence of the country road. Birds circled and screeched in defiance.

'I think I should ride into town.' Robert reached for his hat on the hook behind the door. 'I'll try not to be too long, love. One of the railwaymen will probably ride in to let everyone know what's going on. They'll certainly want the list of names of those presently working on that new section of line. I may be able to help.'

CHAPTER NINE

MIXED EMOTIONS

Beth greeted Robert as she erupted from the Royal Hotel entrance. The bar was not yet open, but she'd seen him walking down Mary Street from the window of her street-level private room. She'd watched the street for hours, hoping he would come. Her hair swung wildly loose around her shoulders and her face without makeup looked as pale as her hair.

'Rob, have you any news? Is Ed all right? We've only heard rumours so far, but one of the riders who passed through town a couple of hours ago said he's heard the accident is serious.'

'I'm sorry. I've heard nothing first-hand myself. I'm thinking I may have to ride out unless one of the railwaymen gets here to tell us what's happening.' He fanned his face absently with his hat. 'I know it's useless to tell you not to worry, but I'm afraid all we can do is hope for the best until we hear otherwise.'

He meant his comments to be light and comforting, but he heard her sharp intake of breath and knew she was crying. He moved closer to embrace her, wordlessly expressing reassurance.

Fyre was stabled as usual behind the alley. The number of people milling aimlessly in the street surprised him. Anxious voices questioned him and many pieces of useless information were shouted back and forth.

First reports had been of a mine cave-in followed immediately by news that everyone travelling in a railway cart had been killed. Robert fervently hoped that the truth was somewhere in the middle. He'd certainly not heard any mine news since the riot.

They heard hoof beats long before the rider came into view. The whole body of people moved in one wave of humanity and surged towards the trail to the north.

'Give him room! Give him room!' someone called as the brown stallion snickered and pawed the ground. The rider dismounted in a flurry of dust and haste and was immediately swallowed up by a press of questions and noise.

'*Quiet*! Let him speak.' Robert's ears rang with the violence of his shout, but the crowd gradually settled.

'There's two dead and three goin' to Maryborough hospital. The skip overturned on a join in the rail line. They were all catapulted down a gully. Word is the line will still push on to Gympie. They still want it ready sometime next year. I'm David Gregory, by the way. Newest member of the Maryborough team. I'm sorry I have to bring bad news.' Breathing heavily, he gasped. 'I … I … have the names of the deceased if …'

Beth screamed from somewhere nearby. She was hidden by a crush of people. Robert moved to her side. He drew her into his arms. 'Is … is Edward Kildark one of the dead?' he asked fearfully.

'No, Edward's fine. He's part of the rescue team. The two killed are

Ivan Miscovitch and Peter Walthorpe.'

'Ivan and Peter.' The names were picked up by the crowd and passed down the line. There was a sigh and a moan of shared grief. Both men had been part of the community. They were single but known by everyone.

Robert turned to find Kat behind him sobbing wildly. 'They lived in the boarding house. Nice couple of kids. Oh, they couldn't have been more than eighteen years of age.' She continued to sob and a collective moan of shared pain rolled through the crowd.

Beth tried to keep her head down. She was afraid her radiant face would be an offence to others. 'He's alive! He's alive! Thank God Ed's alive.' Her heart soared with relief. She was ashamed of the leaping joy and tried to compose herself and share in the grief of the others.

Robert continued to hold her protectively to his side. 'It's OK! It's OK!' he whispered in her hair. 'It's OK for us to be happy that Ed is safe.'

Tom Daniels struggled with similar feelings of relief and despair as he reined his horse and dismounted at the crash site.

The square pumper wagon, one side split by the impact of the rollover, lay with twisted wheels across the edge of the rail track. The accident had occurred at the final bend before the end of the new line. Sharp-edged sleepers shone in the sunlight, jutting out into the distance. They waited silently for the couplings to extend them further, into the corridor of specially prepared countryside.

Two dead bodies had been removed to the edge of the clearing. They would have to stay till the police investigation was completed. Blanket-covered, these mounds shared the ample shade of the clustered trees. Red, spotted, and ghost gums grew abundantly.

Tom walked to the shaded area on his right and kneeled beside the dray where three injured railwaymen had been placed. Their heads were pillowed on bedrolls – their bodies lightly draped with a thin cloth. They were quiet and still. Tom, for a shocked moment, thought they were dead as well. Then one stirred and he sighed, relieved.

A makeshift camp had been set up at the accident site – tents, drays, a campfire, tethered horses – even a short line of washing flapped in the sunshine.

Edward Kildark strode through the smoke and dust, looming large and square over Tom's crouched form. 'Hello, Tom. I heard the horse and was surprised to see it was you. These three poor buggers', he indicated the men in the dray, 'ended up in the gully. We managed to haul them up. They're going overland to Maryborough. It'd take too long to organise something by rail. They've got broken bones, but I hope no internal injuries. I'll be riding them to hospital very carefully.'

'How did it happen?' Tom reached out and gently touched one of the men who groaned. He was interested in Ed's reply, but his whole focus of attention was on the injured. He began to run his hands over their bodies to see if there was any further first aid he could administer.

'Ah, word is there must have been a rock or a bit of branch on the sleeper. On that bend, there was no way they could stop.' Edward lowered his voice and whispered, 'Do you know if news of this has reached Gympie yet? I know how worried Beth will be.'

Tom nodded. 'I imagine rumours are flying thick and fast probably all the way to Brisbane. News that you're OK will probably get back just as quickly.' He smiled up at Edward, then reassuringly touched each man's shoulder and began to pray. The rise and fall of the gentle rhythm of his prayer had a soothing effect. One of them joined in shakily with a ragged 'amen'.

A huge dappled grey stallion was backed into the shafts of the dray and all the bolts secured. Edward waved. 'Be back as soon as I can.' He began his long, very slow journey to the hospital. It was more than twenty miles away.

Tom returned the wave and walked slowly and sadly back to the bodies under the trees. 'God be with those who are now journeying and be with us here as we seek Your comfort and peace.'

A strange silence settled on the campsite as all ears strained to hear the sound of disappearing hoof beats and the groaning squeal of the dray's wheels fading in the distance.

Tom began to pray the 23rd Psalm aloud. Many of the aimlessly walking men, their faces still white with shocked sorrow and streaked with dirt, stood now silent and still, heads bowed. The words of comfort resounded, then settled over the campsite like a blanket of healing.

'The Lord is my shepherd; I shall not want. He makes me to lie down in green pastures; He leads me beside the still waters. He restores my soul; He leads me in the paths of righteousness for His name's sake. Yea though I walk through the valley of the shadow of death, I will fear no evil; for You are with me; Your rod and Your staff, they comfort me. You prepared a table before me in the presence of my enemies; You anoint my head with oil; My cup runs over. Surely goodness and mercy shall follow me all the days of my life; and I will dwell in the house of the Lord forever.'

All eyes focussed on the dead. A soft dappled tree shade softened the scene. This time there was a collective 'amen' and the sound of quiet sobs.

Jakdawn, 1881

'It was the most amazing sight I've ever seen. I won't forget it in a hurry.'

The sheet of rains of early February brought an unexpected visitor to Jakdawn. He came with news and returned stolen property. It was early afternoon and a seemingly endless canopy of cloud continued to pour a deluge over the landscape.

'No, I won't come in,' Constable Bart called up to Eliza and Nika on the veranda. He shook the excess rain off his hat and stamped his feet. 'I've left Tige in the top paddock with Robert, but felt I should come down and tell Nika the story in person.'

'Have you caught the men who killed my daddy?' Nika's slight figure emerged fully through the doorway. Her voice cracked in a sob.

'Not exactly.' Sensing disappointment, though he couldn't see her face clearly, he continued, 'No, we haven't caught those men, but they're both dead. We'll never be able to prove what happened, but the man who came to get me is convinced your father's horse had something to do with their fall.'

'Fall?' Nika and Eliza spoke as one.

Bart continued as if they hadn't spoken, 'They apparently fell over the gorge from the trail near Palmer's ridge. For some reason, they had dismounted. Perhaps Tige was giving them trouble. There was a lot of evidence of disturbance and the trail was kicked about. I found their horses standing quietly, but Tige galloped back and forth in an alarming manner rearing up and whinnying. When I arrived he gentled right down, but there was a spark of such knowing intelligence in his eyes. It was scary.

'We found the bodies of the two men at the base of the cliff. I'm sorry to say there was no sign of any of your stolen camp supplies or the gold. The man who found the horses was spooked. He's got this idea the stallion bumped them over the edge.'

'Tige never would have gone with them willingly,' Nika interjected, sobbing wildly. 'He would have … have ha-hated being dragged along like that.'

'Anyway,' Bart continued, 'I brought Tige straight here. I knew it would've been Mike's wish for you to have him.'

'Tige really love-loved my dad. Thank you. Thank you so much for bringing him ho-home.' Eliza gently embraced the sobbing child. They watched the policeman struggle back up the hill through the blinding rain. He slipped every now and then on the waterlogged grass. He'd left his horse free in the top paddock.

Late that same night, the rain stopped as miraculously as a turned-off tap. The night sky blazed with stars and everything smelt fresh and clean. Eliza turned over and smiled as Robert sighed in his sleep in the bed beside her.

She sat up, senses alert. Something had woken her. She couldn't immediately discern what it was.

Then she heard it again. Somewhere in the distance a horse

whinnied. But it wasn't just the horse. There was a human sound – the faraway keening of someone crying.

Eliza moved silently through the hut, trying not to disturb Robert. The timber boards moaned gently, stirred to life by her tiptoed footsteps.

She stood in the darkness, shivering, as she peered up the hill towards the back paddock.

She could barely make out the shadowy figures of the child and the huge shape of the stallion. Then the moon came out from behind a cloud and flooded the paddocks with golden light.

Nika sat on the top rung of the fence, her arms around Tige's neck.

The horse's head rested on her shoulder.

Together they grieved for Michael.

6 August

CHAPTER TEN

1881

'IT'S COMING! IT'S coming!' The crowd surged forward at the sound of the child's excited voice. 'Mummy! Look, it's *so* big!'

The massive black engine, festooned with tiny Union Jack flags and brightly coloured streamers, belched into view. Behind it dragged, in clattering precision, a caterpillar line of shiny timber carriages.

It rounded the bend.

The crowd went wild. They shouted. They laughed. Many danced. Some waved green branches and others threw flowers. They hugged and kissed in wide-eyed excitement. Disputes were forgotten as a huge cheer went up. The noise was deafening – the excitement intense!

Some people had been waiting hours. Now the train was finally here.

After years of planning, delays caused by bad weather, and loss of life, the dreams of many had finally come to pass. The first train from Maryborough to Gympie puffed its way to a shuddering stop.

Carriage doors burst open. Passengers spilled out into the embrace of family and friends. The air was electric with shouted voices and greetings. 'It has been a wonderful experience,' a voice yelled from the midst of the confusion. Many townspeople, railway families, and miners, given the opportunity of going to Maryborough, had travelled back on this first train.

A howl of support rose from the crowd welcoming these people home.

Edward sprang through an open carriage door. Laughingly, he ran towards Beth, who jumped and waved on the narrow platform. He wrapped his arms around her, dislodging her lace-trimmed blue bonnet. They kissed and his voice resonated through her tangle of blonde curls. 'Finally, some time to spend with you. I've missed you so much. I'm sorry to say I've been asked to go back tonight on the ministerial train. They want someone to keep a bit of an eye on the special guests. Don't know when I'll be back again after that. A few jobs in the Maryborough rail yard need attention. Guess it could be a couple of weeks before I'm home to stay.'

He kissed her again and tried to wipe away the disappointment in her eyes by stroking her hair and grinning down at her. 'Cheer up, love. We've got the rest of this day and I don't expect I'll be leaving until very late tonight, not if I know the politicians. They love to hear the sound of their own voices.' He tipped back her head and dropped a kiss on the bridge of her nose. 'One day my wife will come with me and we'll never again be apart for long.'

'Oh, Ed, how much I look forward to that day.' Beth smiled up at him. 'I've got banquet tickets. The mayor distributed a couple of hundred and I managed to get two.'

'Well, at least we can eat. They were supposed to give me a badge or something, but nothing was done. I certainly hope we can get away before all the boring speeches.'

'When's the second train with all the big bods due to arrive?' Beth asked eagerly. 'There's a lot of hungry people wanting to be fed.'

'Aw, all the pollies and their hanger-ons should get here within the hour. They were supposed to leave not long after us.'

'People have been standing here for hours. They certainly must be very hungry.'

'Beth! Beth Masters! Wait for us.' The shout from the far end of the platform pierced the clamour. The steady movement of people continued to spill from the platform and mix with the crowd behind the barriers.

'It's Robert and Eliza.' Edward grabbed Beth's hand and smilingly guided her through the chattering, laughing swirl of people until they finally stood facing Eliza and Robert. Nika hung back, partly obscured by Robert's body, but strands of her hair, caught in the wind, shone golden in the sunlight.

'Hello, Nika,' Beth called cheerfully. 'We didn't see you from the other end of the platform.' Nika's hand fluttered a shy greeting, but she didn't speak and remained hidden behind the adults.

The brief glimpse of the child's face showed stress. She still had a lost and haunted expression. The shock of her father's death was heavy on her heart. She missed her mother terribly. Nika knew it was only the kindness and love showered on her by Eliza and Robert that kept her going. Some days she battled feelings that she would rather be dead – with her parents. But always, always loving arms urged her on.

School was going well. She would never know the full extent of Michael's behest to the Government, but she was able to learn now without interruption. Her ears were deadened to discord or complaint. She loved her lessons. Any prejudice swirled around without meaning. A natural student, she absorbed everything taught. Words were her passion. She lived her life in a world of fantasy and word pictures.

Beth spoke again, 'Come and sit with us at the banquet. It would be good to have some time together. I imagine you have tickets, Rob.'

He nodded. 'All the railway people living in Gympie had first choice and more than a hundred were given out. I just hope there's enough room. The crowd today is larger than I expected. They're certainly not all locals either. I reckon we've even got visitors from Brisbane.'

'At least one anyway.' Edward laughingly pointed to a serious young man furiously writing in a book. He wore a badge stating *Brisbane Daily Mail*.

The rail storage shed beside the final section of line had been miraculously transformed into a banquet hall of inviting coolness and beauty. Hundreds of fronds of greenery lined the walls and a rich smell of gum leaves permeated the air.

Rows of tables groaned with food and drinks. Forms and seating lined the walls and were scattered between the tables. 'They even borrowed some of the desks from school,' Nika said softly.

They moved inside and took up a position near the back wall. The child looked up at the adults and spoke again in a whisper, 'I'm glad we came now.' Eliza squeezed her hand and Robert edged closer to rest his hand on her shoulder.

Crowds poured through the door. Some, still outside, shifted restlessly as a group in front suddenly stopped moving. 'You must have a ticket,' someone called out. 'No one can come to the banquet without a ticket.' A shout went up, 'We've all got tickets, but we've been told to wait. The ministerial train has arrived and no one else is allowed in until all the official party has found a place.'

'None of *them* have tickets,' someone muttered.

A shared moan passed among the hungry, tired people who waited dutifully to let the visiting dignitaries through. There were so many of them! In procession they came – Members of Parliament, their families, friends, and an astonishing number of lavishly dressed society ladies. They swept past the waiting people and into the shed. 'Oh, look!' Nika, shyness forgotten, grabbed Beth's arm. 'Look at that dress. It's the most beautiful blue I've ever seen.'

Beth gasped. 'It looks like silk to me.' She stretched up and whispered in Edward's ear, 'Wow! A bit much for an old railway shed, I'm thinking.' He looked down at her dancing eyes and laughed.

'They all look overdressed to me,' Robert muttered to Eliza.

Suddenly, from outside came dismayed exclamations of disappointment. 'What do you mean no one else can come in? We've all got tickets. The mayor gave us tickets. I don't care how many extra visitors have come. I've got a ticket!'

For a time, pandemonium ensued, but finally the crowd dispersed to return home. Some were very angry. Many were trying to comfort tired, hungry, crying children, who trudged behind them, disappointed.

'I've lost my appetite,' Robert muttered to Edward. 'Can't wait to get out of this place.' He fanned his perspiring face with his hat and sighed deeply.

Eliza patted his arm. 'Let's enjoy the food now we're here. We'll grab a drink as well and then escape out the back before any of the speeches. Perhaps then, anyone still waiting outside could sneak into our places.' She pointed to a rear door partly obscured by a long form. 'I think we could get out. It would be great to walk down and sit by the river before we head home. Go and get some food for yourself, Nika. We'll get some too, then we'll come back here to sit together.'

Beth turned to Edward. 'Are you sure it would be all right for you to leave? No one's likely to ask you to make a speech or anything, are they?'

Edward laughed down into her anxious face. 'No, my love. Now all the fancy folk have arrived from the north they won't miss me at all. As long as I'm on the train back tonight, that's all anyone cares about. You sit here and I'll go with Nika and get sandwiches and cake.'

'I'll help Nika if you'd get the drinks.' Robert sprang to his feet. 'No, don't get up, Liza. You and Beth rarely get a chance to chinwag. We'll get enough for everyone. Then we can hopefully remain unnoticed here at the back.' He took Nika's hand. 'Come on, love, I'll go with you. The crowds are a bit pushy there at the tables. Everyone seems very hungry.'

'I wish they wouldn't all look at me,' Nika whispered. 'Is it because I'm black?'

Shocked, Robert darted penetrating glances around the chattering groups and realised that eyes were indeed turned in their direction. Behind the shelter of fluttering fans, many mouths were muttering and one or two women shuffled uncomfortably in their seats when they saw him looking in their direction.

He nudged Edward. Together the two men turned and smilingly inclined their heads in greeting, then waved extravagantly. Many faces flushed hotly.

'No,' he said to Nika, drawing her closer to his side and protectively squeezing her hand. 'They are looking at us because you are so very lovely.'

She looked up at him and smiled. The girl in the green dress was transformed in an instant from a timid, frightened child into a picture of radiant beauty.

Ed gasped, 'Oh, Robert!' He sighed. 'She really is a beautiful child.'

'And … and I reckon I'd want to kill anyone who ever deliberately hurt her,' Robert muttered darkly. The vehemence in his voice shocked Edward, but when he moved to comment, the man and child were already absorbed in selecting sandwiches and cakes.

'I'll go for the drinks.' He walked to the side of the shed where cups of cordials and water were set out on a long white table.

'Teas are outside,' someone called. 'And … and … celebratory drinks for all ticket holders at the pubs later.'

The official party now sat at a long table festively decorated with green leaves and fern fronds. Edward smiled a greeting as he walked past, cynically observing that most of the assembled guests he had never seen before.

With relief, he dropped down on the form beside the others. 'I've got orange for everyone. I hope that's OK.' They nodded. For a while, they ate and drank in companionable silence.

'Ladies and gentlemen,' a voice suddenly boomed out, amplified by the walls of the shed. The noise awoke the insects and birds outside, drowsy in the heat. A cacophony of sound erupted. Crickets in ear-splitting resonance protested the disturbance. A kookaburra laughed a threatened territorial call. It was picked up and carried from tree to tree until the hut was surrounded with sound. A passing crow cawed his disapproval at what was going on below. A dog began barking furiously in the distance.

'Ladies and gentlemen,' the unseen voice continued, 'I would like to present to you our mayor who will introduce our visiting politicians and guests.'

'And the speeches will go *on* and *on* and *on*,' Robert muttered to Eliza. 'Can we sneak out now?'

They managed to move the form forward, and Beth reached behind and gently turned the doorknob in the door at their backs. It squeaked in protest. The sound was hidden by other noises, and no one turned to watch as they, one by one, carefully filed out, stealthily, through the narrow opening. Surprisingly, the door opened outwards and this made easy access for three boys who responded eagerly to Edward's hearty invitation. 'Come in, there's still plenty of food.'

The five headed across the paddocks to the river. Beth and Eliza found their dragging skirts hampered their progress. They laughed as Nika hitched hers up and tied it in a knot at her waistline. 'Lucky you,' Beth called out, 'you've only got one thin layer. Liza and I have all these petticoats.'

'No, please, Nika, don't take your boots off,' Eliza suddenly called. 'There are too many snakes down by the river.'

The child wanted to argue. She had spent all her early childhood running around without shoes. But the men were already some distance ahead. She smiled back and bounded off after them. They charged through the knee-high grass, creating a clearer path for the others to follow. Sleepy kangaroos bounded away at their approach, and high up in a stand of gum trees, koalas grunted their disapproval at the human interruption.

'It's a pity we couldn't have brought the horse and buggy down here,' Robert remarked to Edward as they swatted at flies with their hats. 'I've left them in the holding yard behind the pub. It's going to be a bit of a slog on the way back.'

'Ah, don't worry, mate. By then it'll be cooler and Beth'll probably want you all to stop for a drink at her place before you head home. I think it'll be very late tonight before that train leaves. I'm grateful she's got her little place right on the main street.'

It was cool on the riverbank and they sat, grateful for the shade, relaxed and lulled by the gentle murmur of the river's caressing voice.

Nika suddenly pointed upstream. 'It was just round that next bend we had our camp,' she said sadly. Robert and Eliza nodded. Edward and Beth exchanged worried glances.

'I'm sorry.' Edward moved to gently touch Nika's shoulder. 'I wouldn't have suggested coming here if I'd known.'

Nika shook her head. 'This river is beautiful and always will be for me. My mother is buried somewhere on the bank beyond our camp. I was born on that same bank. The river is in my heart. It's like a second home to me. I'm glad to be here.' She sat on her haunches and gazed at the ebb and flow of the water. She settled into a position of almost frozen stillness.

Then she bowed her head.

She knew they could not read her face, so she let the conflicting thoughts swirl in her mind. The sorrow for what was past almost consumed her. The pain was real. If it were possible, she would throw away the boots, rip off her skirt, and run and keep on running until she disappeared somewhere out there in the distant bush country.

But she balanced it with the love she knew from Eliza and Robert. She knew she would survive. She had a future. She loved school. She loved learning. Somehow she'd live with the conflict, loss, and pain within her heart.

She thought she heard her mother's voice sighing on the wind. 'Take the love they're offering, my darling,' it sighed, stirring the trees. 'It will be your strength through the years. They're good people. They love you, Nika. They really do love you.'

Nika breathed deeply. She shifted position slightly and her lips moved as if answering an unseen voice.

'It's as if she's praying,' Beth whispered to Edward.

'I think in a way she is,' Eliza interjected. 'In her own way, it's a kind of remembrance and farewell. She's OK. Don't worry. She's dealing with her unhappiness.'

They respected Nika's privacy and talked quietly together, enjoying the peace and stillness.

They stayed by the river for the rest of the afternoon and began the walk back to town in the cool and gentle caress of the late afternoon.

'Please come and have dinner with me,' Beth said. 'It will only be a light meal, but it'll save you cooking when you get back to the hut.'

'Oh, Nika.' Beth suddenly turned to the child, her eyes sparkling with excitement. 'I almost forgot to ask you a very important question. I do hope you'll say yes. Edward and I are planning to be married next year and I would very much like you to be my attendant. Ed isn't sure if he's going to have anyone stand up with him, but I'd surely like you with me.'

'Thank you,' Nika murmured, 'but … but you see I don't really like everyone looking at me and … and I … .'

'You'd be fine,' Eliza smiled enthusiastically. 'I think you'd enjoy it very much and we'd be there to help you.'

'Yeah, kid.' Edward punched her playfully on the shoulder. 'I reckon you'd do a great job. Please think about it. You'd make me feel braver too.'

'You've got lots of time to think about it,' Robert interjected gently. 'There's lots of time. Please promise you'll think about it.'

Nika looked up and smiled at the circle of adults. 'Yes.' She nodded seriously. 'I'll do that. I'll think about it.'

CHAPTER ELEVEN

FAREWELLS – FALL

BETH AND EDWARD, arm in arm, stood and watched the others leave from the end of Mary Street. Robert slackened his hold on the reins and the brown horse settled into a slow amble. It fitted its stride to the gentle movement of the harnessed dray. Nika and Eliza waved from the back and Robert called out, 'Thanks for a great afternoon. Thanks for a good dinner and the drinks. Take care, both of you. Hope to see you soon.'

'See yuh soon. Take care!' The words swirled round them. They waved until the figures were out of sight as they travelled northward on the river road to Jakdawn and home.

'Let's go for a walk.' Edward reached for Beth's tiny hand and clasped it gently in the warmth of his large brown one. They walked slowly, enjoying each other's company, back down Mary Street towards the station. Her skirt brushed the dusty pavement. In the darkness, their attention was drawn to the sounds and sights of lingering celebration everywhere.

'Do you mind living above the pub?' Ed asked quietly as they passed rowdy revellers spilling on to the street. Some were very drunk and becoming loud and argumentative.

'No, love, it's close to my job and everyone looks after me really well. I feel protected wherever I go as folks look out for me. I was glad to have today off, and it was kind of fun to have the others visit my little place.'

The thin dirt track of the main street was alive with traffic. People and horses intermingled and unseen voices called out greetings as they walked. Shanty shops and pavement stalls still operated even though visibility was low and candle lights flickered in a freshening evening breeze. The chill winter's evening had settled already on the town. A few people huddled round an open fire, boiling a billy.

'Would you like a cuppa?' an unseen voice called. 'Thanks, but I have to leave with the train.'

'It's been a great day,' someone else called out.

'Pity about those bloody banquet tickets,' a slightly drunken voice yelled. 'So many people missed out.'

'I'm sorry that happened,' Edward called back. 'It's still been a wonderful day.'

'Do you think the town will change much?' Beth whispered.

'Ah, I think the railway will make a big difference. Let's just hope it'll never lose its heart.'

They walked on towards the station. 'Are you sure you'll be OK getting home again?' Edward asked anxiously. 'It's pretty dark without a moon tonight.'

'I've told you, love. No need to worry about me here. All the folks know me. They all look out for me, particularly at night. They're my family!'

It was after 10 p.m. before the whistle blew and the train began its slow chugging journey back to Maryborough.

Beth cried as she waved goodbye to Ed. She stood alone on the platform, shivering as the wind gusts teased at the collar of her coat and threatened to blow away her bonnet. She waved until his blurred face disappeared into the distance.

She stemmed the flow of tears with her handkerchief, and with her head held high, she walked back, smiling and waving at people until she was safely in her own room.

'I know,' she sobbed into the pillow, 'it'll probably only be a few weeks. But I … I … hate these constant goodbyes.'

How I hate leaving Beth all the time. Edward's thoughts too were sad. He was swamped by a sudden feeling of abandoned loneliness. *I know it'll be different once we're married.*

He turned to the train window and pulled it up to close. Pieces of black coal were already lightly dusting the leather covering of the seat.

He sat down. He relaxed and must have fallen asleep.

The sound of a woman's screams penetrated his mind like a knife. He jumped to his feet.

'He's fallen off the train. Oh God, he's fallen off the train!' The woman continued screaming – a drawn-out terrified, keening wail punctured the night-time peace.

The train shuddered violently and ground to a lurching stop. Edward felt a sharp pain as he was thrown back and his head hit the wooden board above the headrest of the leather seat.

He regained his balance and ran down the corridor to the small, enclosed viewing platform at the rear of the train. Whoever had pulled the emergency cord must have witnessed the accident. Even in the darkness, Edward could still see the crumpled outline of a man's body sprawled across the tracks some 200 yards behind them.

People with anxious white faces leaned out of carriage windows. Someone was already running back along the track. The female voice still screamed. 'He fell out. He fell out,' she moaned. 'I … I … saw him fall.'

Edward moved back inside the train and began to pull frantically at one of the seat backs. He managed to wrench a huge cushioned section apart. Carrying this, he ran along the track and joined the running figure in front of him. 'No, please,' he called back, 'don't let anyone else get off the train. It's too dark and too dangerous. We don't want any more accidents.'

'He's dead! He's dead!' the voice in front of him wailed despairingly out of the gloom. 'I can't find a pulse.'

Edward kneeled on the track beside the crumpled body and put a comforting arm across the shoulders of the young man crying at his side. He reached down to the man who lay on the track, one hand flung lifelessly across the track rail, and checked the pulse. He could find no sign of life either.

'Help me lift him so we can lay him on this seat. We'll carry him carefully back to the train and check him more fully there.'

Edward felt a sticky smear of blood on his hand and could see dark patches dimly shining on the track. The smell of alcohol was strong on the body and even the young man helping to lift was weaving unsteadily as they made their slow way back to the train.

A group of men ran to meet them. They placed the body on the floor of a carriage, between a row of seats. The train resumed its slow chugging journey through the night.

All celebration was gone now. The journey seemed never-ending.

Painfully slow, every mile took an eternity.

It was well after midnight when they arrived at Maryborough Station. Depressed and tired people gradually drifted away into the darkness.

Edward found himself alone now with a dead body in a dark railway carriage. Someone had placed a kerosene lamp on the platform outside and two young people, a woman and a man, presumably friends of the deceased, huddled together in the dim light waiting for the police.

The police arrived quickly. They came on horseback, but behind them in surprising numbers came a surge of curious onlookers. *Even in the very dead of night, word gets out.* Edward's thoughts wandered. The silence of the night was punctured now by the exchange of questions, answers, and the formalities of accident investigation.

When it was over at last, Edward made his way through the darkened rail yard to his hut across the paddock near the back fence. Railway accommodation might appear primitive to some, but the thought of his bunk bed was very welcoming and real. He was aching, tired, and very depressed.

Tom Daniels waited for him, quietly still in the darkness. Tom rose to his feet. 'I heard about the accident. Just came by to see that you're OK.'

He moved forward and lightly draped an arm across the larger man's shoulders. 'Is there anything you need? Have you got plenty of tea and provisions?'

'Yes, thank you, Tom, I've got everything I need. I'm very tired and sad that the day had to end this way. They'd been drinking and I'll always regret I didn't check that everyone was seated before I sat down myself.'

'Don't blame yourself, Ed. Even if you had checked, your job was not to police their behaviour. You were simply asked to return on the train with them.' He reached out and lightly touched Ed's arm. 'Have a good sleep, mate. I'm relieved to see you're OK.'

Tom disappeared back into the darkness and Edward tiredly lurched into his hut and dropped into the bunk. He slept well into the next day.

Unfortunately, newspaper accounts of this momentous day in the history of the growing town were not kind in the reporting of events. The *Mining Gazette* reported a tragic death and the generosity of spirit of the locals who were denied access to the celebration luncheon for the opening of the new railway.

The Brisbane Daily Mail had headlines:

Riot in gold town – Death fall from train.

The accompanying article painted a graphic picture of a wild undisciplined hick town. It described rioting people trying to gatecrash a civic function. Drunken orgies and death at night were all painted from a city perspective with bias against the little community.

Robert fumed. 'One day,' he shouted as he strode across the hut, 'one day this small place will be a thriving city. One day, we'll stand tall among the best of them.'

Eliza and Nika were standing close with arms linked. They nodded in emphatic agreement.

CHAPTER TWELVE

ANOTHER SURPRISE REQUEST

T IGE WATCHED NIKA walk through the schoolhouse door. He
was at the far end of the large paddock adjacent to the enclosed school
area. Neighing excitedly, he galloped, hooves flying, then stood at the
gate nickering. His mane rippled in the sunlight as he waited for her to
walk down the steps. The pebbled path from the bottom of the school
steps connected with the gate of the holding paddock. His eyes focussed
on the swirling dust as his right hoof pawed impatiently at the ground.
Other horses nodded sleepily in the afternoon heat. They whinnied
encouragement. The antics of the large black stallion only momentarily
disturbed their peace.

Suddenly, there were children everywhere. Laughing, talking, schoolbags swung on dusty straps, they poured down the steps. Horses and children performed their daily paddock dance as they reunited. Children mounted, galloped away to distant homes, and called 'goodbyes' as dust spiralled skywards. The ones who walked home wiped perspiring brows, settled their schoolbags more comfortably on their shoulders, and then began the hot slog along dirt tracks and across paddocks. The summer heat bounced back in waves from the ground into their faces.

Finally, the sounds receded into the distance. Talk, laughter, children's voices were replaced by bird calls and the distant murmur of the river.

Tige shifted restlessly. Nika had disappeared back inside. The horse rested his head on the gate, impatient and worried.

'I won't keep you long.' Frances Phillips re-coiled her heavy plait of auburn hair and pinned it more securely on top of her head. She settled back in her chair. Beads of perspiration formed rivers down her neck and gathered between her breasts. She sighed.

The child stood in front of the large desk, her fingers interlaced nervously. Her back was straight and stiff and her golden eyes looked wide and troubled.

'Nika, I'm sorry to call you back. Please don't look scared,' Frances smiled. 'There is nothing wrong. I only called you back because I wanted to speak to you privately for a couple of minutes. Please sit down in one of the front desks. It's too hot to stay standing.'

'I ... I ... thought you were going to tell me I couldn't come to school any more – that there was no more money or that people had been complaining again. Or ...'

'No, Nika. Nothing like that at all. In fact, I had a letter from the Government only this week confirming that you are to be allowed to stay at school as long as you wish. No, I want to talk to you about something else.' She smiled again. Her green eyes struggled to maintain contact with the anxious ones in front of her. 'I want you to consider entering a competition. I believe you have the ability. I ... I'd like to see you have a go.'

'A competition?'

'Yes, a writing competition for all Queensland school children, being conducted by the *Brisbane Daily Mail*. The prize is money, plus an opportunity to select books of your choice – these can be fiction or teaching materials.'

'What … what would I have to do?' Nika shifted nervously. Her ears were finely attuned to Tige's restlessness outside. 'Would I have to write an essay?'

'Not necessarily. The guidelines are open. They want young people, especially ones like you who live away from the city, to write a short story, either fiction or as an essay, truthfully painting word pictures of your life as a school child.'

'Oh … I don't think I could do anything like that. I love words. I love pictures, but … but I don't think I … I could make it into a story.'

'Nika, I know you write stories all the time. You write about the river, the animals, the trees. You make them all come alive. All I'm asking is that you'll think about putting your different images together into a story of about 1,000 words.'

'I … don't know if I could do that. I …' Nika brushed a damp strand of hair back from her forehead. 'I like writing for myself. I love the sound of words, but I don't know if I could make it into any kind of story. I …'

'Nika!' Frances interrupted gently. 'Nika, will you please think about it? Think seriously about it. See what you can come up with and get back to me. That's all I wanted to ask you today. Please think about this and see what you can do.'

Nika rose to her feet. She nodded. Her heavy golden hair fell forward, for a moment, hiding the expression on her face.

She swept the hair back and smiled at Frances. Her skin shone copper gold in the sunlight and her tawny golden eyes met her teacher's with a steady gaze. 'Yes,' she said seriously. 'I can do that. I will think about it and try to write a story.'

Frances watched as the girl raced along the path to where the black horse waited. He pranced and danced as the child wrapped her arms around his neck. Nika must have whispered something in the stallion's ear. Tige raised his head and let out a whinny of the purest joy.

Frances laughed.

She watched them gallop away. The horse and child blended as one. The pleasure they found in each other's company was evident in the beauty and grace of their movement.

'Yes, Nika.' She moved back to the pile of slates stacked on the edge of her desk. As she began to mark them, her thoughts raced on. *I certainly hope you will think about this and try. I know you have much potential. It's an opportunity to show others, particularly that bossy McKeary boy, who still complains about having you in class.*

CHAPTER THIRTEEN

THE WEDDING

A BLAST OF HEAT from an unusually strong westerly wind shuddered against the timber walls of the small St Peter's Church of England. It moaned in the rafters and swirled fine eddies of dust around the feet of the excited congregation.

Reverend John Henry cleared his throat and smiled at the nervous couple in front of him. He extended his benevolent glance over the assembled people and marvelled at how well they had all 'scrubbed up' for the occasion.

Miners, railwaymen, and even old Bert Carlyle, the acknowledged town drunk, looked expectantly at him. Most of the faces were familiar. He waved to the children and nodded in recognition towards the women.

Ed shifted uncomfortably in his dark blue lounge suit. His fingers plucked at the high white shirt front. His chest strained in the waistcoat. He couldn't keep his eyes off Beth. He wondered if she too had sent south for her outfit. He never imagined she could look so beautiful.

She wore a dress of the softest green. Her blonde hair, a piled- high tower of curls, was held by a coronet of real white daisies. A delicate veil of lace fell to her shoulders. The dress had a plain tailored bodice with a line of pearl buttons to the waist. The softly draped skirt fell gently. It exposed only the tips of her brown boots. The dress sleeves were short and she wore light-coloured wrist- length gloves. A green parasol was looped over her right wrist and she carried a small Bible.

Her eyes met his. They smiled. He couldn't believe this day had finally arrived –17 January 1883 – and the love of his life was going to become his wife.

He winked at Nika. She laughed, and he whispered, 'Not long now.'

Nika's attention returned to her responsibilities. She shuffled nervously as she waited for the moment when the ring would be placed on Beth's finger. Only then could she take the Bible, parasol, and gloves.

Nika's dress was simple, a plain-bodiced, gathered-at-the-waist, free-flowing skirt in a golden brown woven fabric with a natural sheen. Its very simplicity highlighted her girlish figure. When she smiled, it was as dazzlingly bright as her hair, which fell in tumbled golden profusion across her shoulders. She looked animated and lovely.

Eliza grabbed Robert's hand. 'Wouldn't Mara and Michael be proud?!' she whispered. Their loving glances quietly reassured the girl.

They all heard a horse's restless snorting with responses from the other animals as a new arrival was being tethered.

After making a frantic dash from Maryborough, Tom realised he was late.

'Sorry,' he called from the doorway as he quickly dropped into a place at the back. Still breathless, he wiped at the dust on his polished riding boots. Ed turned and waved and Nika and Beth smiled. Tom's eyes were riveted on Nika. He sighed. *She is one of the most beautiful girls I have ever seen.* The thought touched a chord somewhere deep within him. He wondered why. Perhaps it was only his protective instinct, but it also brought a sense of indefinable worry and sadness.

Someone at the front laughed. The sound passed and carried until the whole building expanded with the joy of the moment. Vows were exchanged. The familiar beauty of the marriage service ebbed and flowed on the tide of the rising heat haze. Even the timber floorboards appeared to shine with polished approval.

'Ladies and gentlemen, I present to you Mr and Mrs Edward Kildark.' Reverend Henry stepped back and gently nudged the newly married couple forward. Hand in hand, Beth and Ed moved down the aisle towards the door.

Their progress was slow. Every step was impeded. They were enveloped in laughter, hugs, kisses, good wishes, a few jokes, and messages of shouted advice. It was like processing through the embrace of a cocoon of love and well-being.

Tom grinned at them. Excited, they finally burst into the light of brilliant sunshine. The wind and heat for a moment blinded and surprised them.

'It's a disgrace – an absolute disgrace,' an unseen voice bellowed from the brightness. 'Demon drink – a tool to destroy God's plans for mankind.'

'Ban the evil tool,' another voice interjected. 'Stop this blot on society *now*.'

There seemed to be quite a crowd gathered, and once Edward's eyes had adjusted, he was surprised to see some familiar faces.

A huge cry went up. 'Ones who earn their living by serving and selling this evil should be stopped.'

Another voice yelled, 'Barmaid Beth. She's a server of this evil in our midst.'

'Barmaid Beth! Yes! Barmaid Beth' the chant was picked up and carried. 'She's the barmaid server of evil. Barmaid Beth! Barmaid Beth!'

'What's going on?' Eliza gently drew Nika to her side and peered out. Most of the congregation pressed up behind them. A few curious individuals escaped speedily from the back door.

'It's the Temperance League,' Robert stated. 'Most of them are fine citizens, but a few tend to get a bit out of line.'

Tom moved to stand beside Robert. Side by side, faces flushed, and with fists clenched, they prepared to defend Beth.

There was a sound behind them.

John Henry glided with slow dignity towards the door. Authoritatively, he parted the guests blocking the entrance. Then with a sweep of his extended arms, he loudly roared into the sunlight. His deep voice resonated with barely suppressed fury. 'You are *all* on church property. I advise you to leave immediately before I get the law on to you. And … and,' his voice rose higher and higher, 'may I remind you we have just concluded a Service of Holy Matrimony, which is sacred in God's Eyes. What you are doing here is a blasphemous interruption. Go home now and on your knees repent for this disturbance. And may Almighty God indeed forgive you for your scandalous behaviour.'

The crowd rapidly dispersed. A few with heads bowed still muttered, 'Down with the demon drink.'

Beth was clearly shaken, her eyes bright with tears. Ed held her tenderly. 'It's all right, my love. Don't let a few rat-bags upset you. It's OK. It's OK.' He kissed her tenderly and brushed away the tears with his hand.

Eliza, Robert, Tom, and Nika came up behind and formed a circle of protection and care. 'Don't let anything spoil this day,' Robert whispered in Edward's ear.

The whole congregation finally moved towards the canopy where food and drink were arranged on long tables. They were a colourful milling in a paddock of brilliant sunshine. A few of the ladies struggled to anchor large hats. The wind, with sharp, mischievous puffs, kept nudging under the straw brims.

Beth and Edward laughingly moved to join them. 'Nothing, absolutely nothing can spoil this day.'

'Thank you all for coming,' he added. 'Please relax and enjoy yourselves.'

John Henry once more held up his hand. Again he prayed a confirming blessing. 'Grace and Peace be with you.'

'Amen' was the reverent response. 'Now let's celebrate,' someone shouted.

In one accord, guests linked arms and surrounded the newlyweds. 'Whatever the future brings or whatever happens in your lives or the lives of this commune, we are with you and for you.'

A mighty cheer shook the tent. Parrots in the tree outside screeched.

'To Edward and Beth. *Every* happiness for your futures *together.*'

CHAPTER FOURTEEN

VARIETY THEATRE – OCTOBER 1883

Billowing dust blurred the swinging kerosene lamps, and someone sneezed as the mayor walked on stage with an air of pompous dignity. He cleared his throat.

'I'm pleased to welcome everyone here tonight – parents, teachers, children, and the wider community. This literary award is the first to be presented in the Variety Theatre. The winner is … Nika O'Reilly Barritt from Jakdawn Farm. Nika, are you here with us this evening?'

Nika stood, embarrassed. Excitement gave her face heightened colour, and although hot and flushed, she stood quietly, hands clenched at her sides. Her hair rippled across the shoulders of her dark green dress in living golden waves.

There was a burst of applause. Feet shuffled and in one or two places there was an embarrassed cough.

'Isn't that Michael O'Reilly's daughter?' someone from the back called out.

'Yeah, who'd have thought one of her lot could even write their names?!'

Back and forth across the room interjections flowed. 'Bit stuck up for an abo, don't yah think?'

'How did she get to be so hoity-toity?' 'Adopted by the Barritts, I've heard.'

'S'truth, she's a good looker though, that's for sure.'

There was an oath or two and chair legs scratched and scraped on the timber floor.

'*Quiet please*!' Mayor Maxwell Compton glared around the room. 'We're all very proud that someone from our local area has won this award. Nika, would you please come forward now?'

Nika moved towards the few narrow timber steps leading to the stage of the high-walled Variety Theatre. Sounds of revelry and laughter filtered from the drinkers in the Royal Hotel immediately behind the theatre. Only a thin wooden partition separated the two buildings. She smiled shyly at Robert and Eliza, who squeezed her arm as she moved past. Eliza smiled, her face an illuminated mixture of pride, understanding, encouragement, and motherly concern.

'Well, look who's here,' someone called from the back. 'Jeez, mate, you look like you've been riding all day.'

'It's Tom Daniels!' someone else yelled.

Tom stood for a moment at the theatre entrance. He shook loose dirt from his boots as his eyes adjusted to the light. The swaying lamplight inside was much brighter than the gloom in the alley.

He felt like it was the wedding all over again – last to arrive, coated with dust, and barely able to breathe from the hectic rush.

'Congratulations, Nika!' he shouted. He stifled a cough. The dust billowed in clouds as he walked in. 'You've done great, kid!' He smiled, waved at Eliza and Robert, and nodded in recognition of other different faces in the assembled audience. A few shuffled uncomfortably in their chairs.

He reached for a chair in the corner and sank down at the back in the shadows. The room returned to stillness, only punctuated by the gentle flapping of insect wings against the lights.

The mayor ponderously extended his hand to steady Nika as she reached the platform. 'This award is not just a money prize and a book gift prize but so much more. The piece of paper proclaims you as the winner of a colony-wide junior writing competition. It will be a valuable tool to open doors of opportunity for you.' He sniffed importantly. 'Only a piece of paper but valuable in the future.'

'Hope it's worth more than the banquet tickets for the opening of the railway,' someone muttered from the shadows at the side.

'Yeah,' another voice interjected. 'Bloody things turned out to be useless.'

The room erupted with sound. Comments flowed back and forth. Several people stood to hurl opinions across the room. There was laughter, shifting of chairs, and a few ribald curses. Some of the children now ran back and forth, laughing as they scuffed their feet though the dust. Several people sneezed.

Robert sprang to his feet, face flushed with anger. He lifted his fist, but Frances Phillips reacted the fastest. She bounded up the steps and stood beside Nika. Her hand gently rested across the frightened girl's shoulders. She flashed the mayor a glance of apologetic determination, then roared into the darkness.

'Stop it! Stop it immediately. This night belongs to this young person. She has worked very hard for it. She deserves it! She's a creative and talented student of mine and you should all be very proud that she lives in your community.

'You should be ashamed of yourselves. This night is *her* night. It's got nothing to do with you and your upsets. It's all about Nika and her success.' She swiped away tears which threatened to slide down her face. She glared into the half light at the sea of upturned faces.

In the surprised silence, someone called, 'It's Frances Phillips. She's the schoolmarm.'

The mayor regained authority by shouting into the assembled gathering, 'It gives me much pleasure to welcome to the platform Miss Frances Phillips, Nika's teacher.' The theatre erupted with clapping. 'I would like to personally congratulate Nika on her achievement and invite Frances to formally present her with the prize.'

He handed Frances an envelope and stepped back.

With her arm still across the girl's shoulder, Frances walked to the centre-front of the stage. 'This gives me the greatest pleasure. I'm so proud of you! Congratulations, Nika!' She lifted the envelope high in the air so all could see. 'May you continue to enjoy writing *all* the days of your life.' She passed it over to Nika and the two embraced, excited and smiling happily.

The applause was thunderous and a few people stomped their feet in excitement. One lone voice muttered darkly at the back, 'Not bad goin' for a black gin, I'm a thinkin'.' The rest of what he might have been thinking was interrupted. A heavy hand descended, none too gently, upon his shoulder. He turned and the threatening expression on Tom Daniel's face silenced him for the rest of the evening.

What an evening it turned out to be! The celebratory party in the small back room rivalled in sound even the drunken merriment of the pub next door.

'It's been the most exciting night of my life.' Nika was the central figure in the group as they poured back into the alley when all the festivities were over. Still animated and thoughtful, she commented, 'My mum and dad would have been so happy and proud.'

'Are you going to stay overnight with us?' Robert smiled at Tom, who was engaged in conversation and laughed with Ed, Beth, and Frances.

'Thank you, Rob, but Beth and Ed have invited me to stay with them this time. Now they've bought land near the town heart they've got lots of room. Frances is not going home tonight either. I'm going to pitch my tent on the riverbank.'

'You know you're welcome to stay with us any time, don't you, Tom?' Eliza interjected.

'Yes,' said Nika eagerly. 'It's always fun when you drop by.'

Tom smiled widely and with exaggerated politeness took off his hat and made a deep bow. 'I thank you, ladies and gentleman. It would be my great pleasure to stay with you next time I'm here in Gympie.' They all laughed.

When they reached the corner of the alley, Beth, Ed, Frances, and Tom turned into Mary Street, leading Tom's horse beside them. Robert, Eliza, and Nika moved towards the holding yard to collect their horse and dray for the drive home.

Voices called greetings as they walked. 'Congratulations, Nika.

Well done, girlie!'

Robert recognised Kat's voice, but they only saw her give a brief wave before she stepped inside her home.

Nika walked between Rob and Eliza, her face radiant. *First time I've felt life really mattered in a long, long time.*

'I hope this award *will* open doors for you in the future,' Robert's voice broke the silence. 'We want you to have all the opportunities your father would have wanted.'

Eliza moved closer and hugged the girl to her side. 'Darling,' she said, 'we're both proud of you. But more than anything in this world, we want you to be happy.'

Nika hugged them. 'Thank you. You've given me a chance for that. . I love you very much.'

The night was still and cool now. Overhead the sky, a canopy of stars, lit up the red ribbon road before them. Somewhere in the distance a dingo howled. They sang as the dray bumped its slow way back to Jakdawn and the welcome embrace of their warm beds.

Was this indeed the beginning of Nika's new life?

CHAPTER FIFTEEN

PICNIC – STORY SUCCESS

TOM TETHERED HIS horse beside the other grazing animals and walked between the parked drays. He fanned his face with his hat as he moved towards the river. Sunlight sparkled on the blue ribbon of water and a symphony of bird calls resonated from the treetops.

'Cooee! Cooee!' he called. 'Where are you all hiding?'

'We're over here.' Beth and Ed appeared from further along the bank. 'We've set out some picnic blankets in this flat area between the trees.'

'Hi, Tom.' He broke into the clearing and acknowledged with a grin Eliza and Rob's smiling greeting. Suddenly, he saw other faces he knew. He smiled and waved. Fran came into view. She was surrounded by several young people. Tom assumed they were Nika's friends.

Then Nika came dancing towards him, laughing. 'Tom, Tom,' she called, 'I'm so happy you can be here.'

'Happy birthday, kid!' He embraced her warmly. 'I feel like an old man now you're sixteen.'

Rob overheard and laughingly responded, 'Enough of that, young Tom. I wouldn't mind at all still being in my early twenties like you. Come and have some damper and cake and there's fresh tea in the billy.'

Smoke spiralled upwards from the small fire in the centre of the group.

Tom pulled a small brown package from inside his riding jacket. He handed it to Nika. 'This is for you.'

She pulled a beautifully carved polished timber box, with a fold-back lid, from the packet. Inside were sheets of fine white paper and envelopes. There was an ink bottle and a black screw-top pen. 'It's a fountain pen,' he whispered. 'I ordered it from Sydney.'

Under the lid in fine gold lettering was printed: *Nika O'Reilly Barritt.* Nika's eyes flooded with tears as she held the box tightly in her hands. Her head fell forward and the mane of her golden hair rippled in shining strands, obscuring her face. 'Oh, Tom. It's absolutely beautiful. Thank you so much.'

As people gathered around, Rob and Eliza moved to stand beside her. 'What a lovely gift,' Eliza remarked. 'Thank you, Tom. We thought a picnic by the river would be nice to celebrate a mild winter and our hopes for good crops in the spring and summer. Nika's birthday is a special part of it all.'

Sunshine, flowers in the girls' hair, damper, and cake – Nika's memories of the picnic would always remain clear. There were smiling faces, ball games, folk dancing, sunlight filtering between the trees, and the dappled shade cast on picnic blankets and reclining people. Laughter mingled with bird calls and kookaburras loudly proclaimed their territorial rights with laughter of their own.

Tired and happy people mounted frisky and excited horses as the day drew to a close. The walkers strolled in groups back to the town centre while creaking drays began their lumbering journey back to outlying properties.

'Tom is staying with Ed and Beth tonight,' Rob remarked as they journeyed back along the river road to Jakdawn. 'We'll be seeing him sometime late next year, I expect. He's offered to help for a few days.' Rob caught the radiance of Nika's smile. For a moment, a shadow of concern touched his mind.

'As the day is drawing to a close, we're goin' home, we're goin' home,' the Barritts sang happily as the sun slowly set and the evening shadows lengthened.

Nika sat by the window later that night as happy thoughts mingled with memories of the day's events. *It's been a great day. How thankful I am for my life. Mum and Dad, you will never be forgotten. Every year, you're still so real in my heart. Eliza and Rob, I love you very much.*

On her lap, she held the treasures of the day, some gifts of handkerchiefs and flowers, and a pure white stone collected from the river's edge. In the centre, she held the beautiful box Tom had given. *Oh, Tom.* An awakened clear thought in her mind shocked her. *You understand me. You connect with me. Thank you for this beautiful present. It will forever be my treasure.*

'Take care, my darling. Take care!' That night Nika dreamt of her mother.

1886

COUNTRY QUEENSLAND WRITER HAS STORY PUBLISHED IN *BULLETIN* MAGAZINE

The *Gympie Miner's Gazette* carried a simple byline sent to them by the *Brisbane Daily*, which received its information from Sydney by telegram. This news finally filtered through to Jakdawn, when Jake from the next-door property returned home from a week's work in the mine.

'Nika O'Reilly Barritt officially now a published writer. Oh darling Nika, we're so proud and happy for you.' They danced, arms linked, round and round the hut.

The town in various ways celebrated the success of one of their own. Then as the days continued, all the busy chores and responsibilities of the seasons ebbed and flowed in natural progression.

Nika continued her studies. Now that she had officially left school, she studied further with Fran as her tutor.

'What a wonderful life!' When chores for the day were finished, she would sit on the hut veranda and write her stories, while the river murmured gently just beyond the boundary gate. 'I'm grateful for everything.'

If Nika ever felt there was something more she wanted, at this time, she was unaware of it. Writing was her passion. She couldn't even imagine how Tom's return would change everything.

CHAPTER SIXTEEN

NIKA AND TOM 1887

'NIKA, NIKA, NIKA!' The words rang like a symphony in his head as Tom galloped towards Jakdawn. A strong, westerly wind scattered leaves and dust before him. Warm spring sunshine flooded his face with light. He anchored his hat more securely.

'Only another mile to go,' he shouted to the open air. The horse pricked up his ears and neighed an appreciative response. *It's been a whole year since I've seen them. Nika turned seventeen this week. I wonder if they know I'm coming. News in town is that the Barritts have another son. How many changes in only one year!* He laughed. *It will be good to see them again.* Only in the secret depths of his heart was this leaping certainty … *Especially Nika.*

The hut looked the same. The paling fence was perhaps bleached a softer grey, but the snaking river was as blue as ever. Even the grass, scorched brown by winter frosts, was greening to life by the blessings of early spring rain.

Tom carefully closed the top gate behind him. On sudden impulse, he sent the horse to joyful freedom in the paddock and began to walk towards the hut, his swag slung across his shoulder. The edge of a brightly wrapped birthday present poked from one end.

Then he saw her.

She stood on the hut veranda, an all-brown indistinct shape in the shadows.

She looked up. Her eyes widened in excited surprise. Even in the distorting glare of the blinding sunshine, she realised who it was. Her heart leapt.

'*Tom!*' The shock of her shout set up a frantic exchange of bird calls that brought the bush to chattering animated life. A kookaburra, high in a gum tree on the riverbank, began the deep-throated cackle of his warning territorial laugh. From trees everywhere, laughter rang back and forth until a crow overhead cawed loudly. His raucous cry silenced the discordant clamour into muted chirping conversation.

'Tom!' Nika ran now towards him, her loose hair streaming behind her – a river of yellow gold in the sunshine. She clutched at her dragging skirt so she could move freely.

Tom gasped at the picture before him – long, slender brown legs, brown boots, swirling skirt, the gentle swell of her young developing body beneath the pearl-buttoned blouse, and the absolute dazzling radiance of the smile she beamed in his direction.

She ran straight into his arms. 'Tom! Dear, dear, Tom.'

O God, he thought. *I need to be careful here. She's still very innocent and very young.*

But she was softly vibrant and warm in his embrace. His senses reeled, his whole body stirred, desire flooded over him, and blood pounded in his temples. 'Nika, Nika. It's wonderful to see you,' he breathed raggedly into her hair.

Eliza stood with Robert, watching from the veranda, a small baby cradled between them. 'Oh, be careful, darling Nika. Be very careful.' For some reason she couldn't quite define, the sight of the couple's passionate greeting filled her with momentary concern. 'Rob,' she whispered, 'she's still not much more than a child. I hope we've been good parents. I would hate to see her hurt.'

'Ah, Tom's all right. He's a friend of the whole family. I don't think there's anything more between them. Come on, love, let's walk down.' He carefully took her arm. He was still dusty from his work in the fields, but his eyes shone and his smile was warm and welcoming.

'Kettle's on!' he shouted as he walked with her down the few steps, across the path, and opened the house gate. Eliza too smiled, but there was still gentle restrained concern in her expression.

'Welcome, Tom! It's great to see you, mate,' Robert bellowed heartily.

Hand in hand, Tom and Nika walked to meet them.

'This is young Matthew,' Rob said proudly, as Eliza gently pushed back the wrapping to reveal the tiny face of the sleeping baby. 'He's only six weeks old.'

Tom smiled down at the sleeping infant and silently prayed, *Lord, be merciful and keep this little one safe from the dangers and illness of this world. In Jesus' Name.*

He smiled at Rob and Eliza. 'Praise God for his safe delivery. I'm pleased to see you all looking well and happy.' He released Nika's hand and embraced them warmly, gently careful not to wake the child.

'There's something for you here, Nika.' He swung his swag on to the path and with a little bow presented her with the brightly wrapped box. 'Sorry, I missed your birthday, but I couldn't get away earlier in the week.'

'Oh, Tom, thank you. Thank you very much.' The box was filled with writing paper, pencils, ink, and pens. On the very top was a small brown leather diary engraved in gold: 'Property of Nika O'Reilly Barritt'. 'It matches the carved box I gave you last year.'

She turned and embraced him enthusiastically. 'It's perfect. I'll treasure the things you've given me always.' She kissed him on the cheek.

The thought crossed his mind how much she'd changed in the past year. Gone was the child. Here indeed was a beautiful and very desirable woman.

'I hoped you would like it' was all he said gently.

'How long can you stay?' Robert led the way into the hut as he pushed the few scattered chairs into a semicircle so they could all sit comfortably. The kettle was already boiling on the fire, and Eliza passed Matthew into Robert's arms as she began making the tea. Nika placed a plate of biscuits on the table.

'I've got a week off, but I … I'm certainly not intending to impose on you folks for all that time. I'm here to help you, Rob, if there's any work round the farm. Last time we made a great team repairing that back fence.' They both laughed, remembering. Every day they had been interrupted by a late afternoon storm, and on the last day they had stood back proudly admiring their finished work when a bolt of lightning split the giant ghost gum on the riverbank. One of the massive branches fell on the fence and smashed it into a crumbled mound.

Nika laughed. 'I remember how furious you both were and then we all couldn't stop laughing. Tom, are you going to camp out again in the shed? Do you have everything you need?' She smiled at him, her eyes shining. 'It's great to have you here again.'

'I've got everything I need. I won't get in your way. I'll join you all for the evening meal, if that's OK. I'll sleep in the top shed and help wherever you need me.'

Eliza handed him a mug of tea. 'Nobody's getting too much sleep around here at present.' She smiled in the direction of the baby. 'But you're certainly welcome to stay and I've got plenty of supplies. You don't ever need to eat on your own.'

'Perhaps we could go for a picnic one day? There's a beautiful little sandy cove about a mile north of our end paddock. It's a shady spot with plenty of space for a picnic. I found it when I was walking a few weeks ago.' Tom's heart raced as he saw the eager enthusiasm in Nika's smile.

The beauty of her tawny golden eyes caught at his breath.

'I'd really like that', he stuttered, 'if … if it's OK with everyone else. I'm happy to be here to help with farm work. I didn't really come for a holiday.'

Robert laughed, 'There's so much around the place you can help me with. But I think it'd be a bit much to expect you to work all the time. Sounds like a good idea to me. You'd better plan to go while the weather's keeping fine.'

'I think it would be great for us all to go,' Eliza suddenly interjected. 'It might be a bit far for the baby in the heat, but if we leave in the cool of early morning, it would be a pleasant walk.'

'Yeah, I like the thought of a break from routine.' Robert smiled across at his wife. 'I'll help you, love. We could make a day of it. Come home when it's cooler too. It'd do us all good to get away from chores for once. Make it Thursday and then Tom can have an early night before he heads back to Maryborough on the Friday.'

Nika sprang to her feet enthusiastically. 'I'll start planning what we can take in the hamper.'

The afternoon was spent catching up on all the news while Matthew slept on the floor beside them.

Thursday dawned clear and bright. The sky was an achingly blue canopy of cloudless beauty. The sun was already warm on their shoulders as they walked. It was still very early morning. The air hummed with the deafening wake-up chorus of bird calls. Magpies, kookaburras, crows, and flocks of parrots on the wing, all heralded the new day with noisy enthusiasm.

'It was a shame the others couldn't come,' Tom said as they carefully wound their way down the grassy bank to the small sandy beach on the river's edge.

'Yes, Matthew had such a restless night. I think they were all just too tired.' Nika smiled at Tom. 'I hope you won't find it dull with only you and me.' She reached across and gently squeezed his hand. She was surprised to find it trembled slightly.

'No' was all he said softly. 'I think it could be kinda nice, just the two of us.'

It was a wonderful picnic. Nika spread the cloth across the sand where the overhanging trees cast their shadows, and they ate and drank and laughed and talked as the hours of the day slowly melted away. 'Are you doing any writing?' he suddenly enquired.

He watched her face as it transformed into animated loveliness. 'Oh yes,' she said, her eyes shining. 'I'm writing stories all the time. Life is good and I'm very happy.'

She stood up and did a little dance; her skirt swirled round her ankles and her booted feet tapped out a rhythm. 'Life is good and you, Tom, are so much a part of it. You, dear Tom, give meaning to my life. You have always been encouragement and inspiration.'

Unlacing her boots, with a jerk she finally wrenched them off. She hitched up her skirt and anchored it somehow on one hip. Then she ran joyfully into the river. She kicked and splashed, laughing and uncaring as showers of water cascaded all over her blouse and skirt. 'Life is good. I'm so happy to be here with you.'

For a long time, Tom was unable to move. He couldn't keep his eyes off her. Beneath the water showers, her smiling face laughed back at him. He wanted to touch her. How much he wanted to touch her. 'I love her. I know I love her. I'm overwhelmed with love for her. I want to touch her. I want to hold her. I want to feel her next to me and never let her go.' He knew he wanted even more than that as desire rose in a tide of passionate longing.

His face was hot, his breathing ragged. He tried to sit very still.

This is not what's best for her, he said inside his head.

But she called out to him now, 'Come on, Tom. The water's lovely.' She began to scoop up handfuls and threw them in his direction, laughing at him. The sunlight and water on her golden hair sparkled like flecks of precious stones.

He slowly removed his socks and shoes. Then on sudden impulse, he dropped his trousers and ran down to join her in his underpants. He prayed the cold water would quell his physical need.

He waded into the river, keeping a safe distance. *Please don't come any closer to me*, he prayed. He splashed her with water and watched entranced as she, in her turn, discarded her skirt on the sand beside his pants. Then she looked across at him.

He saw the love on her face as she surged through the water towards him. Her white blouse was soaked, the swelling of her young breasts now clear and defined.

She ran straight into his open arms, and he reached out and tenderly touched the hard nipples as her body connected with his and their lips met in a passionate kiss. Neither of them wanted to pull away now. 'Oh, Tom,' Nika moaned gently. 'I love you very much.'

'I love you too,' his husky voice breathed into her ear. 'Nika, I love you.'

His hands now caressed her body, and the water lapping gently against them wooed them closer – ever closer together.

He picked her up and carried her on to the beach. He removed his shirt. Tenderly, he moved to lay her on the sand. He placed his shirt beneath her head. Her hands reached out and cupped his face. She could see sparks in the depth of his eyes. 'I love you, Tom,' she said again as she surrendered to him.

Gratefully and passionately, he accepted her gift and their bodies came together and lay entwined by the river. Sandy beach, golden sunshine – for this moment in time, it was as if the world stood still.

'My darling Nika, I love you. I think I have loved you from the time I first met you.' His laboured breathing stirred the strands of golden hair that still trailed across his chest. They held fast, bound in an embrace. She nestled into his shoulder.

'Tom, my dearest, dearest Tom.' Nika's eyes mirrored the depths of her soul. They were twin pools of passionate love. 'You are the love of my life. My darling Tom.'

They lay on the sandy strip beside the gently murmuring river as the afternoon shadows lengthened and the first stirrings of an early evening breeze shivered the leaves of the ghost gums.

Nika moved and stretched.

Tom shifted position and their gently entwined legs unfurled. It was a flash – only a moment in time – and the thought caught Tom unawares.

How dark her leg looks next to mine. It was an unexpected intrusion into the beauty of the day. He was shocked. *I wonder how this would affect my ministry if I had a part-Aboriginal wife.* He hated prejudice in others, but there it was. The thought was there, in him.

Nika looked up. She smiled a dazzling smile that touched the sparks of fire in her tawny eyes. Her eyes met his and hesitated. She knew instantly something was different. 'Tom,' she said softly, 'what's wrong, darling?'

'Nothing, love,' he replied absently. 'I was just beginning to get a bit worried about the time. I don't want Robert and Eliza to be concerned.'

Their clothes were dry now and they dressed and began to pack. Nika wanted Tom to say something – anything. But he had gone strangely quiet, and she didn't know the battle in his mind was more self-loathing than anything to do with her.

They began to walk back across the paddocks to home. He held her hand tenderly and smiled at her, but his thoughts were far away.

He seemed preoccupied.

Suddenly, Nika stopped. Her back stiffened. She drew back her hand.

A thought hit her blindingly, suddenly clear. She screamed at him. Her eyes flashed. 'It's because I'm coloured, isn't it, Tom? Because I'm black you've suddenly realised I'm not good enough for you.'

Tears started from her eyes and streamed down her face. She stood in front of him and he acknowledged with shock he had never looked at the face of a more beautiful woman.

'How could you? How could you have ever told me you loved me?' Now she pounded violently at his chest. 'Tom, how could you have done this to me?'

'I love you, Nika.' Tom struggled to gain control of the situation, but within himself was the battleground of his own surprising prejudice. He needed a bit of space to sort it through. 'I love you with all my heart. You are the most beautiful and wonderful person I have ever known in my life. I have never loved anyone the way I love you. Something tells me I never will.'

'But … but what would your mother say about your wanting to marry an Aboriginal whore? What would all your fine church madams say about your marrying someone like me?' Bitterness rose now in Nika's heart, and she spoke savagely with a ferocity that belied the 'falling to pieces' taking place inside her.

'Get on your horse, Tom Daniels. Ride out of my life and never come back. I'm Nika O'Reilly Barritt. I'm proud of who I am. I'm proud of my parents. I don't need you. Get back to where you've come from.'

'Nika, please. Please, Nika, don't go off like this. I love you. Truly I love you. I … I, darling, give me a chance to think.'

'It's all right, Tom. You love me, but what a great pity it is that I'm *not* white,' she spat the words at him. 'Now let's go back and join the others. We can tell them what a great picnic we've had. Then you can wave cheerfully and ride off tomorrow. If you come back again, I'm going to make sure I'm not here.'

'Nika!' Desperately, Tom moved to bridge the gap between them. 'We can't let this end this way. Perhaps today should not have happened. I take responsibility for it. But, my dearest one, I do truly love you. What happened was special. It cannot end here. I love you too much. I love you deeply, sincerely. We cannot walk away from this.'

'Oh yes, we can, Tom Daniels. Don't forget I saw your face. I'll not forget the shadow on it. You love yourself more.'

Together, they walked back into the hut. Tom placed the picnic basket on the table and stood silently by the door.

'I'll take Matthew so you can get dinner.' Nika moved across the hut, tenderly taking the infant from Eliza's arms. She smiled happily at Robert standing near the fire.

'Did you have a good day?' Robert asked cheerfully.

'Great!' Nika and Tom said in unison. Their faces radiant appeared happy and unconcerned.

From this time, none of their lives would ever be the same.

CHAPTER SEVENTEEN

BRISBANE, 1888

THE STREETS HAVE certainly improved though they are still very narrow. Tom's thoughts flowed as he guided his horse and sulky along the dusty road. *Even street signs with names of kings and queens.* He smiled. *This place has certainly defied the odds and is expanding fast. Three separate communities, but the city heart is still growing.*

The capital city of the colony of Queensland was regarded by many in the south as only a village. 'Little more than a garrison town emerging from the shadows of its convict past.'

Convicts were moved away in 1839 and land sales began in 1842. Drought, illness, and ravages of animal diseases brought hardship and sorrow, but the spirit of development and growth remained strong.

Tom felt the evening chill on his face as his eyes looked at the buildings around him. The Majestic Theatre was nearly completed while many structures dotted around were still simple wooden buildings. The stone foundations of Parliament House and the Customs House proudly affirmed their permanent intentions.

Tom manoeuvred his carriage between other parked vehicles, tethered his horse, and walked up the two steps to the temporary city reception hall.

*Quoted from the Australian Encyclopaedia. Printed by the Grolier Society.

'Here's Tom now." His mother moved to the door with the gliding grace he remembered well. The hem of her elegantly styled blue gown brushed the wooden floor. She was, as usual, surrounded by beautifully attired women who followed in her wake like fluttering butterflies.

Tom saw his father and other menfolk standing against the back wall. Their faces wore masks of stoic patience.

'Welcome home, darling.' She embraced him as he mumbled a reciprocal greeting in her hair. 'We're all happy you're back. There are great opportunities for you to minister here. Many church buildings are under construction. I'm sure there'll be a position for you.'

He was jostled and swept into the room. Sophie Jacobs grabbed his arm. Blue eyes sparkling and blonde hair swinging, she laughed as she gazed fondly up at him… 'Glad you've come to your senses. Brisbane's the place to be, not some "hick" mining town in the bush.'

His father called from across the room, 'Good to see you, Son.' Then, smiling, he strode with outstretched hands to warmly embrace him. 'Hope you are doing OK.' He spoke quietly into his ear, 'Don't become a prisoner to what is expected of you.'

Tom grinned at him. For a moment, the two men shared rare closeness.

It was planned as a night of celebration. A young pianist called Pete provided music. Whether you sat and listened or danced, there was ample food and drinks set up on tables against the side wall.

The air was filled with music, laughter, and the sound of constant chatter and greetings.

The night passed in a blur for Tom. He felt suffocated by the press of people. The excess social gossip penetrated his mind with intrusion.

'Dance with me again, Tom,' Sophie simpered. He politely and carefully guided her on to the dance floor and steered between other couples. She smiled up at him, her blue eyes expectant and contented. His mind was far away and his feet moved automatically.

If only Nika were here with me now. The thought came with blinding clarity. It shook him. It was powerfully real. He felt he had been propelled back from some distant place. *If she were here beside me, I could handle even this.* He gasped. A tear trickled down his cheek. He swiped at it.

'The music *is* beautiful.' Sophie danced on, radiantly happily. 'Oh, Tom! Tom! I'm pleased you're home.'

The oppressed feeling of suffocation intensified. *I've got to get out of here. I've got to get away.*

He found his mother and father and thanked them for the evening. 'I'll ride out to see you tomorrow. I'm very tired. I've got a bed at the Alfred Hotel.' He left them, aware they looked after him with enquiring glances. He knew in another moment they would be happily surrounded by friends.

At the door, he said a polite goodnight to Sophie and dropped a kiss on the top of her immaculate and shining hair.

'Oh please, Tom, don't go!' She reached out and grabbed his arm. 'I'm sorry, Soph. I feel I simply don't belong here anymore.' He hugged her and continued walking.

'Good night, everyone,' he called back. 'It's been good to see you all again. Thanks for coming.'

He slowly moved into the street and returned to where his horse patiently waited. He unhitched the animal and carefully guided the horse and carriage between the many others clustered outside the hall.

Suddenly, blinding streetlights dazzled his eyes. He gasped. 'They've turned on the electricity.'

Everything was transformed. The river (also called Brisbane, as a tribute to the Governor of N.S.W., Sir Thomas Makdougall Brisbane) was touched with shafts of light, from places where previously the gas lights had only dimmed the gloom. It looked beautiful.

Tom drove on, awed by this new beginning for the developing city. *One day, it will be incredible.*

He didn't stop at the Alfred Hotel as he had planned, but moved further down the road to where he had seen the small wooden outline of a little church he had passed on his way into the main street.

Sounds of laughter and music followed him, but it was still and quiet in the little churchyard. He parked under a huge Moreton Bay fig tree. The sign on the fence read 'St Andrew's'.

Once his horse was again tethered, he walked between the many tombs. Headstones shimmered eerily in the dim light.

The door of the small wooden building creaked open. Tom stumbled inside. He dropped to his knees in the aisle. Six rows of pews on each side towered over him. The cross was a simple wooden attachment on the end beam of the church. Light from outside filtered through the windows and subdued the total darkness of the small church's interior.

'Oh God, please help me. I don't know what I want to do. I feel directionless. I don't want to be here. I've come home, but it doesn't feel like home. I don't belong and I don't really want to. I feel lonely and adrift. I know I love Nika, but I accepted it when she said our relationship was a mistake. How could the love we felt be wrong? She said she didn't really love me. Said she was too young. My career and my life would be ruined. My mother has continued to reaffirm this. And … yet … yet this longing for her, and for a different life, is strong.'

Suddenly, something like a revelation or a bolt from heaven hit him. He never could describe what happened, but from his knees he fell prone on to the floor as sobs racked his body.

'My Lord,' he cried, 'I once said I only wanted Your Will for my life. I think I have been driven by what I want. I want Nika even if she doesn't want me. I want to marry her and I don't care what the conventions or society may think. My Lord, forgive me for wanting my

will and my way. Help me. Please help me to find what it is You want. Is it here? Is it far away?

'Heavenly Father, lead me, direct and guide me. Make me truly Your servant. I'm confused. Help me to find the full purpose for my life.'

How long he lay in the darkness or how long the crashing waves of grieving broke over his soul – or even exactly why the grieving was so intense – would never be known or understood.

He wasn't expecting an answer except, perhaps, through the Word, but what came was clear. It shook him – more powerfully than anything had shaken him before. Clarity was like the rushing breath of God's Spirit over his life. It wasn't in his ears but deep within his heart, and it pierced his mind. It penetrated like an arrow into his body and his soul.

'Return to Gympie. Trust Me! Among the fringe dwellers and the broken, you will find your place. Nika will be by your side, but you will have to work to find healing and forgiveness. The struggle to make this relationship right in My eyes will be worth the effort.'

CHAPTER EIGHTEEN

GYMPIE, 1889

'GOD HAS A purpose for this community.' Tom's voice rose with emphatic emphasis over the heads of the jostling Mary Street crowd. 'He has a purpose for every one of you. You are not an accident. The formation of this community is not an accident. Our Creator God will bring us through to fulfil our destiny.'

Soft falling rain descended almost unnoticed on hats and shoulders. After the intense heat of early morning, it was a welcome relief. People smiled as the men flicked it off their beards. Women and girls brushed down their skirts, while some little children stomped boots in the thin trickle of water. The street was slowly being squelched into clay. A few horses not left in the holding yard raised their heads and whinnied delight at the refreshing shower.

The street was unusually busy. There were many visitors from neighbouring boroughs. Not everyone stood listening to the young evangelist. He yelled his message from a slightly raised platform wedged between two open street stands of fresh produce.

Horse riders with accompanying dogs and the usual press of pedestrian traffic still went about their own business preoccupied and largely disinterested.

The smell of smoking, damp wood from a few open fires permeated the air. The spluttering sound was a gentle background blur to the shouted human voice.

'Jesus Christ was sent by God to show us the way. He …'

The Salvationist band somewhere further down the street suddenly intruded with a loud trumpet blast and human voices began belting out the strains of 'Onward Christian Soldiers'.

A swelling chant rose from the strong Temperance representatives scattered through the crowd. 'Ban alcohol – the devil's tool! Ban all alcohol! Ban it now! Pour it all in the river!'

A scuffle broke out and a drunken reveller lurched into the people, arms swinging. 'Ban you lot!' he roared belligerently. 'Throw everyone of you'se in the river, that's what I'd like to do.'

Tom yelled more loudly. He was irritated by the interruptions but stifled any hint of anger from his voice. Rivers of perspiration ran down his cheeks and he occasionally clenched and unclenched his clammy fists. 'Jesus came to preach moderation in all things. I'm here today to tell you He came to show you a better way to live. His is the way of love and peace. His is the example we should follow. He died that we might live better lives.'

'We are not divided, all one body we,

One in hope and one in love and one in charity.

Onward Christian Soldiers marching as to war

with the Cross of Jesus going on before.'

The singing voices came nearer as one of the crowd loudly shouted, 'Alcohol is the devil's brew.' He was unceremoniously shoved into a street-stall awning.

'Look out!' Beth screamed to Ed as they hastily stepped aside. The timber awning crashed into the street and several cabbages splattered into the mud and rolled away.

Then Ed looked up as a horseman dismounted further down the street, tethered his horse, and strode towards them. 'Beth! It's Robert. He looks very angry. He's carrying a rifle.'

'I've never seen Rob with his rifle in town before.' Beth moved closer to Ed and clutched his arm. 'I hope nothing's wrong. He hasn't been to town for ages, and it's weeks since I've seen Eliza and Nika.' Robert's mind was full of images. His glance flicked across the people to settle on Tom smiling benevolently at the crowd. As he continued preaching his sermon of love and life, Robert's finger itched to blast the smile from his face.

It was nearly three months since he had found Nika, her arms wrapped around Tige, at the back paddock gate. Her green dress was stained and her face ghastly white from blood loss and pain. His horrified eyes were barely able to grasp a truth he hadn't even suspected. 'I … I was pregnant, but I think I've lost the baby, Rob' was all she could gasp before she collapsed into his arms.

She'd been too ill to move and Dr Judd had prepared them for the worst. He'd ridden out to the hut on numerous occasions. 'She's very ill. She has a severe infection and very high fever. She may not make it.'

'I'm sorry. I'm so sorry,' Nika would moan into the darkness. 'I've let everyone down.' She was anguished and often flailed around violently in delirium. 'Tom, Tom!' she sobbed. 'I love you. I thought you loved me too.'

Gradually, as her health improved, the whole story came out. Eliza sat beside her bed, encouraging her to talk but never pressured her to confide. Often there were hours of silence. Matthew usually played on a rug beside her.

Not even the child's laughter reached Nika. She retreated into a kind of depression. She shared about the time by the river. 'It was special. It was very special. It was my fault – all my fault,' she moaned. 'Tom was not to blame. I love him. He said he loved me too.'

'I can fix her body,' Judd remarked once despairingly, 'but I can't fix her mind or soothe her spirit.'

Nika broke her silence one afternoon. She softly shared with Eliza. 'Tom said we would be married. I believed him and felt it would be right. But … but that was before I saw the expression on his face. I… I will never be able to forget the way he looked at me. He suddenly noticed how brown my legs were beside his. A kind of shutter came over his eyes and his smile vanished.'

In the weeks before Christmas, Robert and Eliza had been concerned as they witnessed what they thought then was the breakdown of the special friendship between Nika and Tom.

Tom rode out frequently, supposedly to help with farm chores. He always seemed his usual cheerful self, but Nika had refused to see him. They'd asked her what had destroyed the friendship. She had replied quite matter-of-factly, 'Oh, we're still good friends, but I'm too busy now with my writing.'

One day, Rob found Tom calling through the hut window, 'Nika, please. Please come out and talk to me.'

Her passionate reply had been emphatic. 'It's better, Tom, if you just go away and *never* come back.'

He left town. Word spread he had returned to Brisbane and was not coming back.

When the full story was out, Eliza and Rob understood something of Nika's pain and heartache.

'I'm really not good enough for him,' she told them both one night. 'I'd ruin his ministry and his life. It's 'cause I'm black, you see.'

Then she had turned and sobbed bitterly into her pillow. 'I love him very much. But in the eyes of everyone, I'm just an Aboriginal whore not worth anything. I wish I'd died with my mother and father.'

Robert had been deeply stirred. A fierce anger welled up as he suffered with her. He held her, cried with her. 'Nika, you are beautiful. You can be anything you want to be. You will have money. Your father safely invested for you. You can do things. You can make a difference in this world.'

She had sobbed, 'Without Tom, nothing has any meaning.'

He should not have let it happen, Rob thought now. *We trusted him. We welcomed him into our home. He knew how special Nika is to us both. How could he hurt her this way?*

Tom's passionate voice rose in intensity, 'The world needed a Saviour and in the fullness of time God sent His Son and the gift of salvation and forgiveness is available to all. That's what's so amazing about grace. It's a free gift.'

'I want to talk to you.' The depth of controlled anger resonated with menace. Robert's voice soared over the heads of the crowd.

It drew attention away from the fight further down the street between a group of rowdy drinkers and several vocal Temperance advocates. The Salvation Army band's rendition of 'Onward Christian Soldiers' continued to resonate with enthusiasm while a couple of dogs howled support.

'Now!'

Several people shuffled nervously. Tom looked across the assembled people. Robert's appearance shocked him. He was surprised by his rude and angry interruption.

'I'll be finished in a minute, Rob,' he gently responded. He cleared his throat and smiled an invitation to all. 'Come this day. Open your hearts. Jesus is waiting for you to accept Him as Saviour and Lord of your life. Come.'

'Tom, I *will* talk *now.*'

Edward and Beth came up behind Robert. Beth reached out and squeezed his shoulder. 'Hi, Rob,' she said cheerfully. 'Haven't seen you in ages. Hope life's treating you well.'

Edward thumped his back. 'Good to see yuh, mate. Bet you're pleased about the work commencing on the new Brisbane–Gympie rail line.'

Rob nodded. His grim expression never lost its focus on Tom's face. His body was stiff and he still held the rifle clutched against his chest.

Ed had never seen his friend this angry. He was reluctant to speak but needed to break the tension. 'Everything OK, mate?' he asked gently. 'Anything I can do to help you?'

'My business is with *him*!' Robert's finger pointed angrily towards Tom, who now, with a smile, wended his way through the crowd to their side.

'Hello, folks,' he said cheerfully. He extended his hand. He was hatless and the damp and wind had plastered his hair into a sandy golden cap. Damp with perspiration, his green eyes still danced. He looked the picture of youthful innocence and vitality.

Robert hit him.

His fist came up and connected with something solid. Tom lost his balance. He wavered for a moment, then fell heavily on his back to the street.

A howl went up from the nearby onlookers, 'Fight! Fight!' And the crowd scattered. Parents moved to take their children to safety while others jostled to get a closer look.

'Someone's hit young Tom,' a voice behind a vegetable barrow informed all who would listen. 'Looks like that Barritt bloke – the one from Jakdawn. He's the one who's hit him.' The information moved in a muttered wave down the street. 'Rob Barritt's just punched young Tom.'

Beth reached and carefully removed the rifle from Robert's now more relaxed grasp. She passed it to Ed, who stowed it behind a tub of tomatoes at a stall being erected behind him.

Except for the tight, curious circle of onlookers, most people had returned to shopping. The band had taken up a position halfway along the street and the fight was subsiding into restless mutterings. 'Devil's in the drink. Booze is the curse of us all.'

Passers-by were now more interested in joining those peering anxiously down at Tom splayed in the sodden clay.

Slowly he sat up. Robert moved towards him and lifted his fist as if to hit him again. Beth and Ed moved quickly. They grabbed his arms.

'Come on, Rob, this is not the way. Let him up. Whatever's the matter? Please let him up and let's talk.'

Beth was near to tears as she reached out to Tom. 'You OK?' she asked anxiously.

He shook his head at her proffered hand and slowly, unsteadily, scrambled to his feet. His shirt and pants were splattered with mud and his boots had small clumps of clay on the laces. His face was white as he turned to Robert and anxiously asked, 'What's wrong, Rob?' The sick dread in the pit of his stomach already warned him of the answer. Somehow Rob must know about him and Nika.

Restlessly, interested bystanders pressed forward. 'Is he up?' 'Why'd Rob hit him?' 'What's happening?' 'I can't see. Quit shoving.'

A sudden heavier shower of rain scattered the crowd. Kat Caruthers appeared at Beth's side. She was dressed impeccably in a purple dress of rich brocade – the lace at neck and wrists elegant and expensive. Through the mud splats, her black boots still shone with polished brightness.

'Hello all', she called cheerfully. Her smile was wide and welcoming. Her red hair coiled high and enclosed in a white scarf bounced lightly as she moved to stand in the centre of the small group. 'Been watching from my window. Not a bad sermon, young Tom. Think you've got a lot of convincing to do among this lot here.' She waved her hand in the general direction of the street.

She focussed her gaze upon Rob and her concerned eyes met his. 'Don't know what's your problem, but I've come down to ask if you'd like to walk back home with me. We'll all have a cuppa and you can get away from the eyes of this curious lot.'

'No use smirking at me,' she called across at a bearded brown shape lounging against a dray beside a vegetable stall. 'I know you too well, Hank McGregor. You love a fight and can't wait to get involved.' She linked her arm firmly with Tom. 'Come along, young Tom, walk with me. You lot can follow us.'

Bemused, Beth stepped between Ed and Rob, joined arms with them, and dutifully fell in behind the tall figure, whose purple skirt brushed the roadway. People parted as she walked regally through.

Everything happened too fast for Robert. Somehow Ed now had his rifle. Bile of helpless anger still rose in his throat. He felt ill. Only the evidence of grazed knuckles convinced him it wasn't all a bad dream.

Tom would remember the pain, anger, dawning understanding, and self- condemnation that flowed during this afternoon with friends. He was shattered by the grief he had caused. He believed that in time forgiveness would come. He knew his relationship with the Barritts would never be quite the same. He explained with total honesty his intention to return permanently to Gympie and his prayer for reconciliation and a future with Nika.

'I was intending to ride out and see Nika today,' Tom quietly said later.

'No! Not today. Perhaps in a couple of weeks, but be prepared she won't want to see you.' Robert's shouted response revealed to them all that healing of his anger would take a long time.

On his knees that night, Tom prayed. *Forgive me, Father, for the pain I've caused to others. Help me to live in Your will and purpose. I love Nika. Give me Your Wisdom and Divine Grace to help her understand this. In Jesus' Name. Amen.*

He tossed and turned in his hotel bed that night and only the assurance of God's grace and forgiveness gave him hope for the future.

CHAPTER NINETEEN

THE LEGEND OF KAT

ONE AFTERNOON IN early spring, Kat Caruthers stood outside the Royal Hotel.

A Cobb and Co. coach thundered into town. The wheels sloshed through the light rain and clay. This time it did not bring a passenger but came to take one home.

She knew when no passengers disembarked and recognised the head and shoulders of the driver with his long, bushy black beard that this coach had come for her! Kat wished she could run, but knew she would not get far. *This time in Gympie has been like a dream.*

The coach door opened.

Strong arms reached out and hauled her inside. 'Katherine Jane

McAlister, it's time to come home.'

The horses had slackened pace but now galloped at breakneck speed back down Mary Street out on to the river road and on to the main south road.

Who was Kat Caruthers? Katherine McAlister? Katherine Macguire? Was she really a duke's daughter? Convict governess to the governor's children? Even perhaps a royal mistress?

Rumours gave her legend status through the decades. Some believed she was the escaped mysterious wife of a South Australian pastoralist. What was she doing in Gympie? Why did she come? Was she a brothel madam? A boarding house accommodation provider?

Many, various, and complex were the stories that filtered back in the following years, but for those who had regarded her as friend she would always be remembered for her kindness.

'I'll never forget her,' Beth confided to Ed. 'Who and where she came from or is now is not important. She will be forever part of the fabric of our story.'

Kat too smiled back at her time in the small roistering gold-mining town.

'Thanks for the memories.'

CHAPTER TWENTY

REJECTION

NIKA AND MATTHEW heard the approach of a horse and rider. 'Perhaps it's Mummy or Daddy.' The child pointed excitedly at the distant figure.

'No, love, they're helping Mr Jacobs with his back fence. I'm not expecting them home until just before dinner time.'

The man dismounted at the top gate and carefully replaced the bar.

Nika forced a smile for the child's sake. When she heard the galloping hoof beats, she knew who it was. Her heart raced but felt like a stone within her. Rob had warned her Tom was back in town and she had desperately hoped he would come. Yet she dreaded what they would say to each other.

Tom rode carefully down the steep hill. He reined in with a flourish at the fence surrounding the hut. He freed the horse and the stallion snickered excitedly and galloped away, weaving and darting in exuberant leaps in the sunshine.

'Nika! Oh, Nika!'

She didn't answer. He opened the fence gate, taking special care to fasten it again securely. He knew it protected the child. He walked on. There were only three wooden steps separating them from where she stood on the veranda and where he had stopped on the dusty pathway. It felt like a mile. She stood still like a marble statue, shoulders squared, head held high. Her golden eyes bored into him, hiding all expression. Her mouth was compressed into a firm straight line.

'Hello, Matthew Barritt, me lad. I'm pleased to see you again.' Matthew laughed, delighted.

'Say good morning to Mr Daniels. He went away to live in Brisbane. It appears he's come back to live again with simple people.' Her voice was as cold as her expression, but Matthew didn't notice.

'Good morning, Mr Daniels'. He danced up and down excitedly. 'Would you like to see my soldiers?'

Wordlessly, Nika stepped aside as Tom and the boy surged up the steps and across the hut to the child's partitioned-off sleeping area. They sat together in front of the line of tin soldiers proudly marching across a long plank. Someone had placed it under the timber-slatted window.

'Would you like a cup of tea?' She didn't look at him, simply threw the question into the empty air.

'Thank you, Nika. That would be great.'

Matthew clapped his hands. 'Milk and biscuits for me, please Nika.'

Her expression softened as she smiled at her little brother. His blue eyes shone and fair hair fell in spiky disarray over his forehead.

She kneeled to rekindle the wood fire. It was still encased in a stone recess in one corner of the kitchen. A new hammered plough shear made an effective stovetop. The flames leapt and the simmering kettle stirred to a rolling boil.

She made the tea and brought the milk and biscuits from the hanging cupboard.

Tom tried to look into her face, but she turned away. He took the child's hand. 'Let's go and wash our hands, then come back and sit with Nika. We'll play with the soldiers later.'

He returned from the water pump and stood for a moment, holding Matthew's hand. As he stood framed in the doorway, Nika looked up and saw him for the first time. His boots were dusty and his shirt and pants crumpled. His eyes were clouded with tiredness and he looked sad with a droop to his normally erect shoulders.

His expression broke through the sharp edge of her hostility. 'Please sit down,' she said gently. 'Take the window seat and I'll sit with Matthew on the chairs.'

He took a step towards her. 'Nika … I … please, can we?'

'No, Tom, please. I don't want to talk about anything now. Please sit down.'

'*Matt*! Only one biscuit at a time.' She moved the plate out of the child's reach and sat in the handmade timber chair beside him.

She looked across the table at Tom and his heart turned over.

Still as lovely as when he had last seen her, she wore a dress of deepest blue. He wondered if materials and dresses still came from her grandmother in Ireland. Even after stoking the fire, she looked cool. Her delicately arched dark eyebrows highlighted the tawny depths in her extraordinary golden brown eyes. Her scraped back hair, pinned up in piled-up confusion on top of her head, shone with hidden lights like a halo. Her expression was closed – unreadable.

The neckline of her dress was open and the skin on her throat and face had a dusky, burnished copper sheen.

He swallowed.

For a moment, their eyes met.

He smiled. She didn't return the smile. 'Nika, I've come to ask for your forgiveness.'

She still sat ramrod straight. Slowly she sipped her tea. She focussed on Matthew, whose top lip was coated with milk. He was restless, eager to be back playing.

Realisation stabbed Tom to the heart like a knife – the woman in front of him was a different person from the child-woman of their recent past. She was harder. There was defiance about her. This woman was Nika O'Reilly Barritt.

There was a wider gulf between them now than the one his imagination had forged. She was confident. Money gave her not only education but also lifted her from one status level to another. She had control of her own destiny. He felt humbled yet strangely exhilarated by this certainty.

He ached to reach out. He wanted to wrap her in his arms. He longed to wipe away the pain of hurt he had caused. *Oh God, I believe I would give my life to protect her. I love her more than I ever believed possible.*

'Please, please come and play with me.' Matthew was beside him now, grabbing at his hand. 'The soldiers are going to battle.'

Smiling but reluctant, Tom allowed himself to be led back into the child's room.

He looked back at Nika. 'Please forgive me.'

He looks sad. Could we really ever start again?

Tom's voice came to her over the noise of cannon fire and childish laughter. 'Nika, can we begin again and be friends?'

'Friends? Yes, we can certainly be friends. We can't have too many of them.'

She went outside and weeded the vegetable garden while he played happily with Matthew. Her mind was a riot of conflicting thoughts and feelings.

'It's time I was going. I will be back. Nika, I'm permanently here now, and I hope one day you will let me speak to you about how much I love you. For now, I'll settle for friendship.'

'Bye, Mr Daniels,' Matthew called from the veranda as Tom whistled to his horse.

'Bye, Matthew.'

Nika now stood beside the child. 'Bye, Tom. See you again.'

'I don't particularly want to meet up with Eliza and Rob so I'd better go now, but …' He saddled his horse and prepared to mount. 'Why, why, Nika, didn't you tell me about the baby?'

'Tom, do you really think I would try to trap you into marrying me? Would the knowledge of the child have broken through your prejudice? I saw you cringe – draw away from me when the reality of our backgrounds hit you. Then, of course, I knew your mother was totally against even our friendship.'

'My mother? What has my mother got to do with anything?'

'Tom, your mother wrote to me. Shortly after you left Gympie, I received a polite letter from her, telling me that if I really cared about you then I would not allow "our friendship" to get in the way of your future prospects or ministry.'

'Nika, darling, I didn't know. I'm so sorry. She had no right to do that. Nika, I love you. Nothing in this world will keep me from you. Tell me you feel the same and absolutely nothing will keep us apart.'

'Please go, Tom,' she said gently. 'Leave the past in the past. The loss of the baby almost killed me in more than one way. What I did to Eliza and Robert tore my heart apart. Let's be friends and accept that this is the way it is meant to be.'

He waved from the top gate. His stomach was tied in hard knots of hopeless grief. *Will I ever be able to tell her the truth I know in my heart? Without her I am nothing. She alone can complete everything I am supposed to be.* He was shocked to find his cheeks were wet with tears.

Goodbye, my dear Tom. The tragedy is I still love you. I probably always will.

Back inside, the tin soldiers had advanced across all available space. They had even surrounded and captured the sugar bowl in the middle of the table.

'I'm Nika O'Reilly Barritt.' Nika stood to her full height and proudly tossed her head. 'I am Nika O'Reilly Barritt. I will survive.'

She desperately struggled to control the tears coursing down her cheeks.

'Are you crying about Tom?' Matthew asked, his eyes focussed and wide.

'Yes, darling. Nika is crying about Tom. Nika is crying about many things. But …' She smiled at him. 'It's almost dinner time and your mummy and daddy will soon be home. 'I've got to start peeling potatoes.' She lunged and hugged him tightly.

Matthew laughed. 'I love you, Nika,' he whispered in her hair.

CHAPTER TWENTY-ONE

FLOOD

'I'M GETTING UNEASY about all this rain,' Rob remarked to Eliza as they cleared the breakfast table. 'I'm thinking of opening up the top paddocks so the animals can move more freely. The lower paddocks are becoming quite waterlogged. No need for you to come, love. Stay here in the dry.'

Eliza laughed. 'A bit of rain won't kill me, and it will be quicker for you if I help.'

'Nika,' she called, 'we won't be long, dear. Stay warm and dry.'

Nika and Matthew laughed. The hut leaked in several places and everything inside became soggy. It was the time of year for lots of rain, but the fierce storm on Boxing Day which shook the hut triggered a deluge. It was still raining five days later, not always heavy but persistent and uncomfortable.

It was a pale, rain-sodden grey day. Strong wind gusts once again battered the hut. Rain kept driving through the timber slats and formed puddles on the floor. Rob and Eliza had not returned by mid- morning and Nika was becoming anxious.

Her troubled golden eyes could see through the downpour that the river was rising. It had reached the vegetable garden by early afternoon and was edging gradually relentlessly towards the hut.

I feel uneasy. She suddenly spoke aloud to Matthew. 'Darling, I think we should pack a few things and go for a walk up the hill and look for Mummy and Daddy.' She did not want to alarm the child and made a game of it, but she gave him now precise instructions.

'Take the pillowcase off your bed and fill it with clean clothes. Put in socks, pants and shirts, and a pair of shoes. Put your rain boots and coat on now.'

'Where are we going, Nika?' Matthew slipped his hand for a moment into hers. Worried blue eyes saw her concern. 'Can I bring my soldiers?'

'We're maybe going to sleep tonight in the storage shed at the top of the hill. You can't bring all your soldiers. Perhaps you could bring…' She tried to calculate a precise number he would understand. 'You could bring … one … two … three … four … five … six. Yes, you could bring six.'

'I want to bring them all. Please can I bring them all?'

'Matthew darling, grab as many as you can carry and put them in the pillowcase with your clothes. Then bring it to me and come and stand beside me.'

She was puzzled by a sudden desperate sense of urgency that propelled her. She wrenched an old suitcase from under the bed – the only large container she could carry and filled it with an assortment of clothes. She flung in a container of milk powder, tea, sugar, and at the last a small box of biscuits.

'Put your things in here.' She helped the child ram the bag in, and together they closed the lid.

Matthew's eyes suddenly filled with tears. 'Nika, I can't go anywhere without my bear.'

'Go and get Toby! Come straight back. We've got to go *now*.'

The wind outside the hut was stronger than she expected. Sheet of rain drenched them in seconds – their waterproof coats useless now against the strength and force of the rain.

Nika stopped at the top of the first incline. She brushed sodden tendrils of hair from her eyes. As she held Matthew's hand with her left hand, she struggled to drag the suitcase behind them with her right.

This is not ordinary weather. It's much too violent.

They turned and looked back down the hill towards the hut.

For one frozen moment, it was as it always had been – a simple timber hut on the bank of a beautiful river, quiet, peaceful, and safe.

Suddenly, there was a sound like a mine explosion. They watched in horror as a building-high wave of brown water suddenly surged around the bend from upriver. It crashed relentlessly on to the bank beside the hut. There was a howling noise as if a fierce wind had pushed the wave. The wave was alive. It contained a maelstrom of swirling objects. There were pieces of timber, fence posts, barbed wire, sheets of iron, dead animals – sheep, cattle, pigs, large rocks, and incredible boulder-size chunks of earth and shale.

The destructive wave crashed over the hut, smashing it instantly. It then roared across the bank and up the hill towards the shocked figures of the woman and child.

Pieces of the hut, chairs, beds, tables, and loose kitchen items – now part of the river – swirled in coloured kaleidoscope patterns through the dirty brown water.

Nika screamed. She heard her voice above the roar of the river and the noise of the rain. 'Oh God, help us.'

She never knew how they got to the highest point of the back paddock. Instinct drove her to go even higher than the storage shed. She would only ever remember running, stumbling, running, clutching tightly on to the child, and desperately clambering for some high place of safety above the river's violent surge. She kept her eyes focussed always on the highest rocky ledge in the distance. She climbed, lifted the child, and forced them both onwards. She lost her grip on the case when they both fell exhausted to the ground.

Nika woke up stiff, wet, incredibly cold. It still rained in a constant persistent bone-penetrating drizzle, but now it was dark. She had no idea where she was or how she had got there.

'Matthew,' she yelled. 'Matthew, where are you?' Her anguished cries echoed hollowly through a stand of towering ghost gum trees.

'*Matthew*!'

'Nika,' the frightened child's voice answered from very close behind her. 'Nika, I've still got Toby.' A small figure stood up. Out of the darkness, he stumbled, a bedraggled, mud-covered child barely recognisable as a little boy. Tightly clutched in his fist was a cloth bear. The bear now resembled a clump of muddy earth, but he said again proudly, 'I've still got Toby', and fell into Nika's outstretched arms.

She held him, as salty tears of relief and gratitude, mixed with mud and rain, made track marks across her cheek and dropped globules on to his head.

<hr>

Survival

Robert reached out his hand in the dark. It connected with another hand. Leaves, bark, mud, and pieces of broken branches were everywhere.

'Liza!'

She moved and he could feel her pulse. 'She's alive! We're both alive.' His heart soared with gratitude and relief. He struggled free of all the debris and carefully moved to help Eliza into a sitting position. She was cut and bruised and incredibly dirty, but they gratefully fell into each other's arms.

She sobbed, 'We couldn't make it home. What if Nika and Mathew were trapped in the hut?'

Her grief was inconsolable, and Robert answered through his own anguish, 'We had to help that calf. We couldn't leave it trapped in the gully. We had no way of knowing there would be mudslides and slips and we wouldn't get home. Darling, I'm sorry.' His body shook with despair. She held him tightly in her embrace.

In brokenness, she prayed, *Lord God, please help our children. In Jesus' Name. Amen.*

A dark shape loomed above them and the soft nuzzling breath of a horse brushed Rob's ear.

'Tige.' Eliza gasped, 'Rob, it's Tige. He's OK. The other horses seem to have panicked and gone, but he's found us.' The stallion neighed his delight at their movements.

They struggled to their feet. Eliza removed all her mud-soaked outer garments, and in underwear and petticoat she mounted the waiting horse.

'I think it would be better if I lead,' Rob said. 'It's slippery and dangerous, but there's a trail on the ridge that leads to town. Not that there'll be much of the town left if the river's burst its banks downstream,' he added sadly.

They would tell people later it was the longest, coldest, wettest, and most miserable journey of their lives, but the morning light found them high on a hillside.

They had a clear view of the broken remnants of what were once the beginnings of a thriving township. Their shocked eyes could only see devastation.

It would take weeks before losses were calculated, but stories of miraculous human survival became the grist of passed-on generational legacies. Ed and Beth would spend three days on the roof of their partially built hut while Fran and several children were rescued from the school house veranda. Most of the school grounds had been swept down the river. Eliza and Rob had no comprehension the community could one day recover and that once again it would be a prosperous frontier town.

Today, huddled together against Tige's warm side, they grieved.

CHAPTER TWENTY-TWO

DESPAIR– HOPE

Tom Daniels ploughed relentlessly through the sodden paddocks, swiping at the constant rain which battered his face and obscured his vision.

'That's the last of them,' he shouted to his neighbour, Mer, who was balanced precariously on the slippery grass incline leading to his hilltop paddocks.

'Thanks, mate. I couldn't have done this without you. I'll get 'em as high as I can. The river's broken its banks and there's a torrent of water coming from upstream.' The cattle bellowed now as panic spread through the herd. They galloped, their hooves churning up the grass and dirt. They could still be heard snorting and stamping their feet even when they came to the paling and the strung wire barrier fence in the top paddock.

From upriver, Tom heard a horrendous grinding sound. As the grinding and crashing intensified, the noise penetrated and drowned out all sounds of the howling wind and driving rain.

Something is terribly wrong. This is much bigger than simply a flood.

A wall of water hit the lower paddock. It was driven by gale force winds that swirled and tore across the fields. *It's taking everything below the road and sweeping it all into town. Oh God! How much of the mines and township will be left?*

His mind was numbed by the thought. He stumbled back to the highest point and sat on a large rock.

He watched as fence posts were wrenched out and barbed wire rolled away into the whirlpool. A wave of water containing wood, cupboard doors, a hanging basket, and tangled clothes writhed in a maelstrom assortment of mud and weeds. There were bodies of animals and other shapes he couldn't identify.

This wave swirled and sloshed across what once had been green paddocks.

It's right beneath my feet. Tom's thoughts raced as his heart pounded erratically.

Something attracted his attention – a gleam of shiny paint. A small object was wedged and carried by a tumbled mound of muddy clothes. It washed up into a grassy knoll on the edge of the tidal surge. Curious, he climbed down to have a closer look. His foot stirred the flotsam. The small flash of paint disappeared.

He kicked aside a mound of muddied clothing. Again he caught a glimpse of something bright. He scooped up a handful of mud and weeds and felt a solid shape in the mess. He wiped the mud away. In his palm, he now held a hand-painted tin soldier.

Just like Matthews.

Absolute horror washed over him. The realisation this thought generated would be etched in his mind forever. *The devastation must have begun upriver at the very headwaters. What hope would the Barritts have had on the river's bend?*

'Nika! *Nika! No! No!* Please, God, *No!*'

He ran to the roadway and managed to catch his brown mare. She had waited for him and not run free into the hill country. He leapt on her back. The wind howled and tore at his clothes. He put his head down and rode like he had never ridden before. Black despair pierced his soul.

His mare was sure-footed. Carefully he guided her. 'Come on, girl. We can do this.'

Rain teemed in torrents through which the mare slid and struggled. She was sure-footed, and although he guided her carefully, gratitude for her plucky tenacity was high on his mind. The rest of his mind and body stayed frozen with horror and dread.

In darkness, without the light of stars or moon, as rain continued to pour in torrents, he found them. Under a gum tree on a rocky hillside, on the edge of the riding trail, Nika and Matthew sat huddled together, filthy, cold, and very, very wet. They were drinking water from a mug and eating soggy biscuits. A suitcase – battered, broken, and muddy – was a pulped mess at their feet.

'Nika! Nika! Thank God. I thought you were all dead.'

Startled, she looked up at the bedraggled apparition image of horse and rider silhouetted against the night sky. She recognised his voice.

'Tom! How did you find us so quickly?'

He would always believe it was a miracle. All around was carnage. The river would overflow its banks down several miles and wash over and destroy countryside probably not immersed for hundreds of years. The miners' dwellings on the river would be lost and the central township almost obliterated. Temporary shops, pubs, brothels, farm sheds, huts, and many lives would be gone forever. Yet, now, in darkness, he had found them.

He dismounted and ran, slipping and sliding, towards her. 'Nika, my darling! My dearest one, I love you.'

The face through the curtain of darkness and rain was blurred, white, and desperate with anxiety. In a moment of absolute certainty, she knew how much Tom loved her. Her heart leapt to his with the same clear assurance. 'Oh, Tom. Dear, dear Tom, I love you too.'

He dropped to his knees beside them. His frantic glance quickly assessed that both woman and child appeared unhurt. Enveloping them both in the warmth of his heavy coat, he felt wetness as a muddy cloth bear squelched against his chest.

'I saved Toby,' Matthew sobbed. There was a hint of pride in his statement.

Tom kissed the top of the child's damp head. 'Tomorrow we *will* find your Mummy and Daddy. And …' He reached into an inner pocket. 'I found this.' He brought out the painted tin soldier and pressed it into the child's hand.

'I lost my soldiers in the water when I fell over. Now I've got the gen'l back.' Matthew's smile was tentative, but it tore at Tom's heart.

'I'll get you some more.' Tom again kissed the top of the child's head.

'Eliza and Rob were in the high paddocks when the waters came,' Nika whispered loud enough for the child to hear. 'I'm sure they're OK.'

Throughout the long, cold, wet night, they drew warmth and comfort from each other. Torrential, unrelenting rain continued to fall. Around them, the bush and all the hidden creatures settled into an uneasy slumber.

Tom felt Nika stir beside him. He knew she was smiling as she squeezed his hand.

'Please, Nika, let me look after you. Marry me. I want us to be connected for life. I love you more than I ever believed possible. I want you to write and to be in your life all you were born to be.'

He shuffled to relax his body more firmly against the base of the large tree.

Her face was indistinct in the dim light, but there were tears rolling down her cheeks. 'I never really stopped loving you. Yes, Tom, I will marry you.'

In the chilly darkness of their tenuous position, the words rang with a beauty that warmed his heart. They tried to sleep. It wasn't easy, but exhaustion gave them periods of rest.

The first light of dawn filtered through the trees, and the rain had gentled to a steady shower. The struggling sun penetrated some clouds, promising warmth later.

Nika's voice splintered the silence. In her radiant face, her eyes were golden brown pools of fire and excitement.

'Tom, Tom, look up there! Watch the sun catch the light. The treeline comes alive. It's a high ridge – a solid rock escarpment. It forms a huge circle of solid stones. Tom, do you see it?'

He nodded.

Matthew woke and the three now stood together. Tom carefully extended his arms to keep the coat wrapped around their shoulders.

'My mother spoke about the importance of "limga" – rock solid foundations.'

She pointed. 'Oh, Tom, Matthew, look up there! Watch the sun catch the light. It makes the whole hill shine and the rocks glow.'

She stopped. For a moment, she was totally still – as if solidified.

Then she nodded.

As if transfixed by a glorious vision no one else could see, she spoke again, 'Tom, I know, *I know* now what I must do. I have the money. Together, we will build a children's home, hospital, and house up there. It will be a permanent symbol of hope for the whole community. High above the floods on solid rock.

'One day, one day there will be Marranga–Limga. Marranga in memory of my mother and her people and limga – a rock solid promise for the Gympie community. Certain hope for a future.'

Marranga–Limga

Tom waited until there was a break in the rain. Then they stood, arms linked. He prayed, *May this indeed be fulfilled. Nika and I together. Lord, I ask in Jesus' Name. Amen.*

The Promise

Is Marranga–Limga more than the materialistic concept of *hope*? Is it a promise beyond flood, fire, or even earthquake? Is Limga the *Rock*, the one sure eternal certainty?

9 781970 703245